KAYLA WREN

Spring Kings

First published by Black Cherry Publishing 2021

First edition

ISBN: 978-1-8381116-7-0

Cover art by JS Designs

This book was professionally typeset on Reedsy. Find out more at reedsy.com

Contents

Chapter 1

I dunk the nail polish brush in the glass bottle, swirling it around before drawing it back out. Two more careful strokes and the toes on my right foot are finished: wet and shining under the lantern's glow. Emerald green. I blow my hair out of my face and shift on the bench, drawing up my ruined leg.

It's stiff. Scarred. Warped. And it's going to have pretty green toes, damn it.

A breeze drifts through the shadowed gardens, wafting the scent of jasmine over my cheeks. I tip my head back, eyes closed and nail polish forgotten just for a second.

That breeze. After another long, muggy day, with air so hot and heavy you can chew on it—that breeze feels so good it should be illegal. I lift my elbows, holding up my arms so the cool air can reach all the sticky bits.

"Emerald glitter?" I squint one eye open and find our head of security, Jamie, leaning against a statue of a lion. Jamie wears a suit while the lion is dressed in white stone, but they each have matching manes. "What's the occasion?"

I squeeze my eye shut again and go back to ignoring him. Jamie's always somewhere close. Watching. Keeping an eye. Usually I like having him near—like having someone to chat to—but right now my leggings are rolled up on my scars and I'd give anything for him to turn around and sidle back round the ponds.

"Francesca?"

I huff. He knows I hate my full name.

"Doctor's appointment."

Which Jamie knows, because he's in charge of my schedule. Dad has him run this estate like a fine-tuned Swiss clock, all-knowing and all-seeing. And tomorrow, for my appointment, it'll be Jamie driving me into the city.

He hums and pushes off the lion, strolling closer with his hands tucked in his suit pockets. He always dresses flash, just like the rest of Dad's men, but sometimes when he lifts his arm I glimpse the gun holstered under his jacket.

It's kind of funny. I can't picture Jamie ever firing it. To me, he's the man who sits up playing cards on the deck when I can't sleep. Who sneaks me beignets from the best bakery in the French Quarter, and spent nearly twenty minutes scooping out a moth that fell in the fountain.

"It'll come right."

Jamie sounds like Dad when he talks like that, but I don't tell him so. I let him crouch in front of my garden bench and inspect my toes.

While he's looking at the emerald glitter, I inch my injured leg back down to the floor.

"Oh, no you don't."

A warm hand wraps around my ankle and places my heel back on the bench. His grip is firm but not harsh, and he holds me there, the pad of his thumb rubbing back and forth over a scar.

I hold my breath, but it's like he doesn't even realize what he's doing to me. Jamie plucks the brush out of my grip and dips it in the polish, swirling it around.

"Are you worried? About tomorrow?"

A line creases Jamie's forehead as he paints my big toe, slow and careful.

"No." It's true, mostly. I've had a thousand of these appointments. The doctors are just going through the motions at this point, too scared to tell Dad he's fussing over nothing.

I can't blame them. Dad can be fierce, especially when his protective instincts are triggered. And when it comes to my leg, Dad is all instinct. He's just so damn guilty.

"Then why are you sulking out here on your own?"

I level Jamie a glare, but he smirks at my second toe. If he weren't engaged in such a delicate task, I'd thump him on the shoulder.

"Maybe I want to make your job harder. You've had an easy ride of it so far, don't you think? Keeping an eye on the estate and babysitting little ol' me."

"Is that all you think I do?" Jamie asks mildly.

I flick a lock of his red hair, tickling at his collar. "Yup. It's like you retired at thirty-five."

"Thirty-two." He sounds strained.

"Well, I'm just saying. It could be good for you. Sharpening those skills. Like when office workers go on courses about spreadsheets."

Jamie sighs and looks up then, his blue eyes pinning me to the spot. Back and forth, his thumb rubs over my scar. Back and forth.

Goosebumps prickle over my bare arms, never mind the warm night.

"You can hide if you like." His mouth quirks up on one side.

"But you know I'll always find you."

Promises, promises. Dad would have Jamie's hide if he heard him say things like that.

Sure enough, footsteps crunch down the gravel path, summoned by our flirting. Jamie pushes the nail polish brush into my hand and straightens. He's upright and out of reach by the time the footsteps round the fountain.

"Carrick." Jamie nods respectfully.

Me? I poke my tongue out at Dad. He strolls over, his eyes flicking between us, measuring the distance. I'm half surprised he doesn't whip out a measuring tape and make us each hold an end.

Dad is like Jamie: sharp suits and sharp smiles. But older. Harsher. With graying hair and great shadows under his eyes, and plenty of bite along with his bark.

"Behaving yourself?" He ruffles my hair and I nod, though I'm not sure who he's talking to.

"Always."

He snorts. "Now if that were true."

Then what? The question bubbles up in my mouth, but I choke it back. It's not like I'm difficult or unruly. I do my lessons; I get good grades. I'm set to graduate early from distance learning with Llewellyn College next month.

And then what? Really: then what? I've barely left this estate in the last eight years. My big outing is to the doctor each month.

I don't know what I could do to behave better. To earn more trust. Hell, I haven't even jumped Jamie's bones, and the thought crosses my mind at least twice a day.

I can't live the rest of my life in my parents' estate. The damn Siamese cats have more freedom. But every time I bring up looking for jobs, or even taking on a role in Dad's business, it's like I pulled open his shirt and stabbed him straight in the heart.

Not today. I can't have that same argument again. Not with the appointment tomorrow. That reminds me—I dip the nail polish brush back in the bottle and set to painting my last two toes.

"You after your doctor?" Dad eyes my sparkly nails, and I wiggle them. The flecks of glitter catch the lantern light.

"Hardly. He's about a hundred years old."

"Then what's with the fancy feet?"

I shrug. "Distraction tactics."

Dad and Jamie both fall quiet, and I tug my leggings down until they cover my scars. I shouldn't have said that. He already feels guilty enough.

The silence stretches for a moment before he speaks again, and I see Jamie shifting out of the corner of my eye. Jamie's nearly as protective of Dad as he is of me. If Dad weren't such a scary bastard, I bet Jamie would follow him around and paint his toes too.

Loyalty. That's what Carrick O'Brien inspires in his men. Loyalty and a healthy dose of fear.

It's weird for me to picture—like trying to imagine Jamie firing his gun. To me, Dad's a pussycat. He sits down next to me on the bench and rests his elbows on his knees.

The sigh that comes out of him rattles on for half a year.

"You should take a day off."

He hangs his head, rolling his shoulders. This is privileged viewing—none but family and Jamie get to see Dad like this.

Tired. Old. Aching after a long day.

"Soon, Frankie. I promise. But we've got business to attend

to first."

This is not news. The O'Brien family always has business to attend to. It's what I keep trying to wriggle into, offering to shadow workers or intern or do *anything*, just to get involved.

Dad won't have it. He says I'm too pure for the family work.

I say that's sexist bull.

"More meetings?" I ask, because he's tired and I won't kick him while he's down. Dad nods his head, still hanging.

"A whole week of them on the west coast."

Huh. That is new. Our business is usually area-specific. We've got our claws in this city, and in deep, but that's that.

"When do you leave?"

"Tomorrow. Your mom and I will see you off to the doctor, then head straight to the airport."

For a crazy moment, panic claws at my throat. The thought of being stuck here alone, of being left behind—I can barely breathe.

But Dad pats the back of my hand, and it brings me back to earth. They're not ditching me; they're working. Flying for hours to meet with boring business people, then flying back to make big, dull decisions.

I swallow hard. "I'll miss you."

Dad turns and gathers me into his arms, all misty eyed.

"Oh, Frankie girl. We'll miss you too."

Over Dad's shoulder, Jamie watches us both, leaning against the stone lion. It's dark in the gardens, the sky inky black, and the lantern light bounces off his eyes.

It's been a long time since we were left here alone.

I shiver and hug Dad harder.

* * *

The suitcases are packed and ready when I come down the stairs first thing. Two soft leather cases with brass buckles, filled to bursting and leaned up against the wall.

Mom does not pack light. She is a glamorous woman.

Dad and Mom are in the kitchen, their voices drifting through the lobby. It's a vast house, way too big for just three of us since Tommy moved out. Even with Jamie in another wing, most of the rooms go unused—barely walked into except for the cleaners doing their rounds.

Dad says it doesn't matter. It's all about power. Projection. A businessman like him is expected to have a large estate and dozens of staff. Anything less and people will gossip. Respect will be lost.

So, fine. We have all these rooms and then use about six of them all together.

I wander into the kitchen: a huge, open plan room with an island and breakfast bar. There are sofas gathered around a wall-mounted screen at one end, where Dad and Jamie sometimes eat breakfast and mutter over the news. Even the fruit bowl on the counter is working overtime, groaning under the weight of perfect, waxed green apples and ripe peaches and plums.

There is too much fruit in this kitchen for this family to possibly eat. Especially once Dad and Mom set off after we leave for the doctor. I chew on my lip as I snatch up a banana, making a mental note to take some fruit pickings to the goats we keep at the back of the grounds.

No sense wasting good food. And besides, who'll be here to stop me? Jamie? He hates waste just as much as I do.

"You've got your judging frown on." Mom dips her spoon into a bowl of yogurt and honey. She folds it over and over, mixing it in, but never lifts the spoon to her berry red lips.

"This is my resting bitch face." I glance at her, but she doesn't smile. Mom is not a fan of mornings. She droops over the breakfast bar, already perfectly made up and dressed in a floaty silk blouse. Her platinum blonde hair rests in bouncy curls above her shoulders, far more lively than the rest of her.

Dad and Jamie look perkier, no doubt both having been awake for hours already. They're in dark suits and crisp white shirts, leaning against the counters. Dad winks at me as I slide onto a stool, but it's Jamie I smirk at as I peel my banana.

He takes a bite of his toast, studiously ignoring me.

Mom sighs tragically and drops her spoon into the bowl, dusting her hands like she's been tilling soil, not yogurt and honey.

"Are you ready yet, Carrick?"

Dad nods, a mostly full coffee mug pressed to his mouth. He grunts, chugging the coffee down, and slides his phone off the kitchen countertop. A few taps and it makes the whooshing sound of a message sending.

Probably super important. Millions of dollars at stake. Dad slides his phone into his pocket without another thought.

"Be good for Jamie." He ruffles my hair, and I smirk at the man in question over the tip of my banana.

"Oh, I will."

Dad scoffs and breaks off half the yellow fruit, then shoves it in his mouth. "Not too good," he says through the mouthful. "We have cameras, remember."

I roll my eyes at the reminder, but my mood lifts straight back up when I see how Jamie's cheeks have flushed red. That's the beauty of redheads: his every emotion is broadcast to the world.

I love making him glow like a little lava lamp. And he lets me push him so much further when Dad's not around.

Maybe this week will be fun after all. I pop the rest of the banana in my mouth and chew.

"Have a wonderful week, Francesca."

I wince at my full name as Mom kisses the crown of my head. Her perfume envelopes me for a second, and moisture brims in my eyes.

I blink hard. Where the hell did that come from? They're going away on business for a week, not moving to Mars. Even so, there's a lump in my throat as I watch their backs disappear through the doorway.

"They'll be back before you know it." Jamie's voice is soft across the kitchen. "And I'll take good care of you until then."

I bite the inside of my cheek and toy with my coffee mug handle.

"I'm a grown woman. Not a houseplant." He starts to say something else, but I slide off my stool and talk over him. "Let me know when you want to leave."

Because I can't even go to the doctor's alone.

Damn, I'm in a spitting bad mood this morning.

* * *

"Seat belt on."

Jamie lowers into the driver's seat, closing the door with a thump. I bite my tongue to keep from snarling at him—I'm twenty-two years old, damn it. I know to put my belt on.

His eyes find mine in the rear view mirror, and he frowns when he sees the angry set to my mouth. Whatever. I'm not responsible for everyone else's feelings, one hundred percent of the time. I'm entitled to be pissed off, and I tell myself so as I turn my head and look out the window instead.

The estate grounds roll past outside: manicured lawns, pale stone statues and trees dressed in bright spring blossoms. A peacock struts through a flowerbed, his tail feathers swaying with each cocky little step.

I suck my teeth and smooth my dress over my legs. I've got leggings on, of course, covering the worst of my scars, but the morning sun is already beating down on the metal of the car and the extra layer makes my knees sweat.

Jamie interrupts my sour inner monologue, his rich voice carrying from the front of the car.

"Anything else on the schedule this week?"

I huff. "As if you wouldn't know."

I don't come or go from the estate without Jamie as an escort. A bodyguard. Glued to my side and constantly watching for the same men who hurt me all those years ago.

He's protecting me. Keeping me safe. I know that.

Doesn't mean I don't wish he'd leave me the hell alone sometimes.

"You are in a piss poor mood today, you know that?"

I shrug, staring out the window. He's not wrong.

"Everyone's moody sometimes."

"Sure."

"Like you, for example. Remember when that dry cleaner tore your suit?"

Jamie's hands clench around the steering wheel. I stifle a smile.

"That suit was a gift from your father."

"You were spitting mad."

"Wouldn't you be?"

I tug on a lock of his hair.

"No. Suits are lame."

Jamie huffs a laugh, shifting in his seat as we pull through the security gate. There are so many cameras pointing at the big iron gate and its little booth, you'd think we were gunning to host the president. I stick my tongue out at a camera, same as always, trying to figure which of Dad's men must be working today.

The car eases onto the street, and Jamie sobers up real fast. He doesn't mess around and tease out in public. He's on the job, one hundred percent focused. A redheaded terminator. After a while, I get bored with needling him and sit back, squinting at the street through the tinted, bulletproof glass.

Something's different. It's always lively out there, especially as we draw close to the city. There are always old men drinking and playing cards outside cafes; always music playing and dogs trotting past.

But today, there's a kind of spell on the streets. A weird urgency. The crowds are thicker than usual, spilling off the sidewalks into the road. They're all headed in the same direction, hips swinging and heads tossed back laughing, even though it's barely past breakfast.

Jamie curses just as his phone rings. He answers it, pressing a button on the steering wheel as Dad's voice fills the car. They chat about business—nothing interesting, just timings and logistics, and Jamie mentions a parade. Keeping one eye on the back of his head, I roll my window down half an inch.

We're supposed to keep the windows up. Sealed and secure. But Jamie's distracted, and it's like the spell on the city is sparking in my blood too. I want to know what it sounds like out there. What it smells like.

Strains of music wash into the car—not so loud that Jamie's onto me yet. There are pounding drums somewhere nearby, thumping out an intricate rhythm. The people walking down the street fall into the same beat, their arms swinging and hips shaking. Then we round a corner and there's the faint tinkle of piano keys, spilling out an open bar doorway.

Jazz, blues, the steady pulse of club music. It all clashes and blends together in a medley of sound. And over it, the whoops and hollers of the crowd, calling to each other. We're still on the outskirts here, just turning close to the river. And we're driving the same way these people are walking, called towards something.

The car slows at a stoplight, right by a one-woman food stall. She's set up on the edge of the sidewalk, a great barbecue fire burning under a grill of roasting kebabs. Spiced meat and marinated pineapple sizzle on the grill, their scent wafting through the car window and making my stomach growl.

"Francesca," Jamie snaps. "Close your damn window."

I place my finger on the button, but I don't press it. Not yet. I suck in a whole lungful of delicious air first.

My window slides shut, controlled from the front. I glare at the back of Jamie's head.

"Don't be stupid," is all he says.

Stupid? Half an inch of open window, and the smell of street food?

Alert the church elders. Frankie O'Brien has truly gone buck wild.

* * *

Every appointment goes the same.

CHAPTER 1

First: the waiting room. Carrick O'Brien does not scrimp on his daughter's health care, so we're talking chilled water with sliced cucumber and a rack of glossy magazines. I pluck a mint humbug out of the bowl on the receptionist's counter and pop it into my mouth, rolling it around on my tongue as Jamie checks me in.

It's a circus. They know who I am by now. They know why I'm here. And they know there's no damn need.

But I check in, and the young receptionist smiles and asks me to wait just a moment, and we wander over to the hard leather sofa.

"It'll be okay, Frankie." Jamie nudges the back of my hand with his own. "It's just a routine check up."

Clearly I've been drinking my bitch juice today, because I tilt my head and cover my mouth like I'm shocked.

"Really? Are you sure, Jamie? Are you sure that's why we're here?"

His face clouds over and he sits back, slapping open a magazine. Glossy photos of the sun setting over a jungle temple spread open on his thighs. The mint humbug sours in my mouth, and I glare at the pages over his shoulder.

I'd give anything to be there right now. To be anywhere except this same doctor's office in the same part of the city we always go to.

I don't even know what our neighbors look like these days.

"You ever been somewhere like that?"

Jamie shifts, turning the page, but pretends like he didn't hear me. That's fine; I'm being a brat today, sure enough. I nudge him with my elbow.

"Wanna go there with me?"

Jamie's mouth tugs up despite himself. He doesn't turn his

head, but he leans an inch closer so only I hear him when he murmurs.

"Your father would hunt my hide across the globe."

"I'll protect you."

Jamie snorts, the sound loud in the waiting room. I'm deadly serious, but I don't get a chance to needle him about it. The receptionist calls my name and directs me to the doctor's room, and then I'm wandering down the same halls I've walked a hundred times before.

I tell myself I'm limping less these days. You can hardly hear my bad foot dragging over the tiles. But it sounds like the sugar sweet lies Dad tells me sometimes about trips we'll take one day together.

The doctor's door opens as I raise my fist to knock. I turn it into an awkward wave instead, thrown to find a middle-aged black woman in a white coat instead of the usual crumbly old man.

"Where's Doctor Fredericks?"

The woman steps back and waves me inside.

"Doctor Fredericks is on leave. A family matter. I'm Doctor Connolly and I'll take your appointment today."

Damn. A new doctor, huh? That's the most interesting thing to happen to me for months, and isn't that a tragic fact?

"Have you read my file?" This will go a lot quicker if Doctor Connolly's up to speed.

"Yes, Francesca. I'm aware of your father's concerns."

I nod and plop myself down in the spare chair by her desk. There's a bed against one wall, covered in a sheet of tissue paper and with a giant lamp hanging above.

I prefer the chair, if I can get away with it. No need to shine a light on my leg.

"I'll get to the point." Doctor Connolly lowers herself into her desk chair and spins to face me, her chin on her hand. "I don't believe these appointments are necessary at all."

I snort. The doctor raises her eyebrows, but keeps talking.

"It's perfectly natural to feel lingering anxiety after a traumatic event. But I believe you would make more progress, Francesca, in therapeutic counseling rather than with these physical check-ups."

I hum, drumming my fingers on the armrest.

"Doctor Fredericks seems to think I need to keep coming back. He says I'm not well enough to return to full activity."

I've always thought that must be bullshit—people live and work and have *lives* with far worse than a few scars and a limp. But the doctor's always been adamant that my leg could deteriorate at any time. That I could do serious damage if I just swan out into the city.

I don't know. It sounds kind of stupid when I think about it. But with Dad being so scared for me all the time, I guess a little of that fear rubbed off too.

Doctor Connolly levels me with a look. The kind that says: check your bullshit, or I'll check it for you.

"There is no mention of any such concern in your file. Only a note about your psychological state, and your father's wish to limit your exposure to stress."

The sliver of mint humbug sticks to my tongue. I cough hard, working my mouth, and frowning down at my knees.

That's not… no. That can't be right.

"I don't understand," I mutter, voice rough.

When the doctor speaks, she sounds almost sorry for me. Almost, but not quite.

"You're fine, Francesca. You're perfectly well. You need to

get back into the world."

I shove to my feet, staggering into the spiky leaves of a potted plant. I'm lightheaded, the room tilting, and the doctor's voice comes from far away. She keeps talking as she follows me to the door, reaching around me when I can't make my hand grasp for the handle.

The cool air from the hall rushes in as she pulls the door open. Sounds fade back in: the gurgle of a water cooler, the hum of electronics, the murmur of voices down the hall in the waiting room.

"Oh, and Francesca?"

I stumble to a halt in the doorway, frowning back at Doctor Connolly.

"Do me a favor, sweetheart. Tell your father there's no room for threats in medicine."

The door closes with a snap, and I'm left in the hall with the wheezing sound of my own breath. I swipe the back of my hand over my forehead and it comes away clammy.

How did I not see this?

You did, a voice whispers in the back of my head. Because that's the truth, isn't it?

I've known I've been fine for years, but still I let my father lock me away. For my own safety, maybe—but this is no life.

Dad knows that. He sees how bored I am; how tiny my horizons have shrunk. And he paid off a doctor to keep lying to me, telling me my leg could get worse.

I shake my head like I can rattle these thoughts loose. Like I can shake them right out of my ears. But they stay in my head, pounding louder and louder with every thump of my pulse.

You're fine. You're fine. You're fine.

Dad lied.

Chapter 2

I stagger into the waiting room, my gait worse than it's been for years. The receptionist frowns at me, her forehead creased with concern, but I charge past and straight through the automatic doors. The spotless glass hushes to the side, and the moist heat outside is like walking into a wall.

"Hey!" Jamie grabs my elbow, lunging to catch up. Behind him, on the waiting room floor, his dropped magazine is bent and splayed. "Where the hell are you running off to?"

Running. It's such a joke. All of it.

I snatch my elbow out of Jamie's grip, ignoring the flash of hurt in his eyes.

"Don't touch me."

He must know. There's no way he's not in on this. Jamie is my father's right-hand man—the only one he trusts alone with me. There's no way he's not in on the lies Doctor Fredericks has been feeding me.

Jamie clenches his hands into fists then shoves them into his pockets, his jaw tight. He steps in front of me, blocking my path to the car.

"What's going on?"

"Did you know?" I blurt, answering his question with my own. I watch in real time, my gut sinking, as Jamie's eyes widen then his face locks down. He turns to stone, rigid and immovable.

"Come on. We'll talk about this in the car."

I shake my head. It's not just stubbornness; I'm not sure that I can walk right now. My world's still tilted on its axis, weird spots floating in my vision, and my chest feels like it's caving in.

Is this what a panic attack feels like? I don't like it, that's for damn sure.

"Frankie. Come on." He takes my elbow again, and I let him this time. I let him guide me across the parking lot, past the shiny cars and rows of palm trees. There are trellises on the surgery walls, I note absently. With climbing pink roses.

"Easy," Jamie murmurs as I stumble, setting me back on my feet. It's almost a relief when he opens my car door and lowers me into the seat.

He leans across me to clip up my seat belt, and I catch a whiff of his scent. Soap and laundry detergent. That's Jamie: clean, clean, clean.

Just like Carrick O'Brien, since his daughter was attacked. A legitimate businessman now he's cleaned up his act.

Clean men don't need to carry guns. They don't lie to their daughters. The car door closes with a thump, and I rest my forehead on the glass, my eyelids fluttering closed.

I don't even notice we're moving until we're three streets away.

"It'll be okay, Frankie." Jamie says the same words as this morning, but I don't believe him this time. How can I? But I nod and force a shaky smile for the rear-view mirror. I learned some things from Dad, after all.

Like misdirection. Biding your time. Waiting for your

opponent's weakest moment.

So I wait until we pull up at a stoplight in the city. The crowds throng the street, even thicker than before, some of them dressed in huge feather head-dresses. Jamie pulls out his phone and starts tapping a message.

Three guesses who that's for.

I wait until a crowd of people come right past the car, laughing and shoving each other. With my unclipped seat belt slithered back into place, I stare one last time at the back of Jamie's head.

I'm sorry to do this to him, but that's all. I'm not sorry for the rest of it.

I fling the car door open and dive out into the street.

* * *

The chaos is immediate and overwhelming. Bodies push past me—elbows, hips and knees—and the feathers from someone's headdress tickle my nose. Behind me, I hear Jamie's shout and the slam of a car door. Horns blare in the street, but I push deeper into the crowd, crouching low to stay out of sight.

I'm just another twenty-something with wild strawberry-blonde hair and a frazzled expression. Nothing to see here.

Music pounds through the crowd from hidden speakers and musicians. The revelers throw back their heads and laugh, harsh and guttural, and shake their tasseled hips so fast that they blur. My eyes snag on all the colors and movements, and I'd give anything to stop and watch. To soak it all in. To feel myself out in the world for the first time in almost a decade.

I don't. I can't. Jamie is quick and strong, and loyal only to my father. He'll bundle me kicking and screaming back into that car faster than I can cuss out his mother. The back of my neck itches as I duck between two drummers, like I can feel his accusing gaze on my skin.

Sorry, Jamie. I'm not coming home. Not yet.

A shout sounds close to me—way too close—and I push myself faster down the sidewalk. My leg screams at me, my limp worsening with every few feet, and I throw myself behind a stall selling sequined masks, ducking behind the black tablecloth.

An elderly woman with brown skin stares down at me, lips pursed. She raps her gnarled hand against the table, jolting the masks, and I flinch but stay put, chest heaving. Her eyes track over my flushed cheeks, my wide eyes, my hand wrapped around my swelling ankle.

Her mouth twists, and she shifts in her fold-out chair, the metal squeaking. Then she turns back to the crowds flowing past her table, ignoring me altogether.

"Thank you," I hiss, gathering my courage to peek around the table leg. I scan the crowds for a dark suit, broad shoulders and red hair, my heart pounding in my rib cage.

He'll be so damn angry. He won't speak to me for weeks after this little stunt.

Well, you know what? That's just fine. I'm pretty fucking furious myself. I rub soothing circles into my sore leg, my palm sliding over the scar tissue.

Maybe I'm not ready to run the mile. Doesn't mean I should be locked away like some medieval princess.

The crowd flows in one direction: a steady, pulsing stream. They're headed to something, some kind of event, and the smart thing to do is to stay with them. Safety in numbers, and all that. I should try to stay lost in the crowd.

I tell myself to get up. There's no sign of Jamie; there's no reason to linger here on the sticky tarmac. I urge myself, plead with myself, count down from ten. Still I crouch there on the sidewalk.

I can't do it. The colors, the noises, the ache in my leg, the crush of bodies—after years of quiet on the estate, it's overwhelming. Literally. It short-circuits my brain.

My forehead thumps against the table edge, jarring the display of masks. This can't be it for my great escape.

"Time to move on, girl," the old woman says in a gravelly voice. She swats at me with her hand. I scramble back, nodding, too tongue-tied to plead my case, and gingerly push to my feet.

Dancers and tourists flow down the sidewalk. There are a few more stands selling feathers and beads. But no sign of a man with red hair and a suit. I turn in the opposite direction from the crowds and try stepping on my injured leg.

Pain flares hot in the bone, then fades away to a dull ache. Fine. Just so long as I can walk.

I limp away from the chaos, the sounds of the parade fading to a distant roar. The sidewalk turns to cobblestones, and it's harder going on my leg again, but at least it's quiet down here. And cool, too, in the alleys between buildings.

The air changes as I go, turning from baked and still to something fresher. A breeze stirs my hair, washing over my clammy cheeks, and the knot in my chest loosens a tiny bit.

It's worth Jamie's wrath just for this. For ten minutes alone with the quiet streets and the breeze rolling off the river. The water glints silver at the end of the cobbled alley, vast behind the wrought-iron railings.

I limp closer. We went on a river cruise once as a family outing, back when I was a kid. Tommy was there, still young too, and we ate a fancy seafood dinner on the deck. I remember, because I hated seafood back then, and I snuck handfuls into my napkin and dropped it on the floor.

Dad hates wasting food. He'd have cussed me out if he'd caught me doing that.

The memory of the four of us out for a family meal—of being allowed out without having to run away from a bodyguard—it stings my eyes and brings a lump to my throat.

Footsteps beat against the cobblestones behind me, and I press myself against the wall behind a stack of old cardboard. Through a sliver between the trash and the brick wall, I catch a glimpse of Jamie running past the alley.

He's headed away from the crowds, too. I don't have much time.

I push off from the wall and limp faster, headed for the river shore. Cafes and restaurants line the street opposite, clustered with little tables and umbrellas. I limp straight past and cross the road, half expecting Jamie's car to screech to a halt in front of me.

Nothing. Just the tang of smoke and the smell of roasting coffee, and the distant hum of music.

Riverboats bob against the jetty, lurching with the waves. There are tiny boats, barely big enough for ten people, then open-top tourers, all the way up to a fancy cruise boat like the one we ate dinner on once. It's like a building floating in the water, it's so big, and its glass windows are buffed to a shine. Unlike the other big riverboats, this one's not sleek and modern. It's all curls and railings, colonial like the buildings, with a giant paddle wheel fixed on one end and two chimneys shooting up to the sky.

My feet change direction on their own. Huh. I guess I liked

that seafood dinner more than I thought.

* * *

The riverboat is even bigger up close. It towers over me at the jetty, so much my neck twinges when I lean back to see it all. Through the windows and up on the deck, I can make out the bustle of life. Waiters and diners; people wandering the halls. It's an ants' nest, floating on the water.

The waves lap against the stone dock walls, gurgling and sucking. All along the jetty, you can hear the clink of chains and the groan of rocking metal. Seabirds flap overhead, miles and miles from the coast.

I guess they're seeking the American dream, too. I salute the nearest one, hunkered and preening on a street lamp.

The entrance to the boat is a wooden ramp, resting on the dock like a drawbridge. There's a chalkboard sign folded out on the cobblestones, with a list of ticket prices.

I pat the pockets on my white shirt dress, but I already know I've got nothing. Only my phone and an old key chain I like to fiddle with when I get nervous.

As if I've woken it with my mind, the phone starts to buzz against my hip. I fish it out, barely glancing at the name before I swipe to answer.

"I'm not coming back, Jamie. Not yet."

"Francesca O'Brien, I swear to God. You'll send me to an early grave."

Once upon a time, that might have been the truth. Dad was ruthless back in the day. But he loves Jamie like a son, and he knows full well what I can be like when I set my mind to something.

Even if I haven't been wilful in eight years. Damn, where have I been?

"Just don't tell him."

Jamie sighs, long and hard. I can hear the pound of his shoes against the pavement through the phone. He's still running, looking for me, though he's hardly out of breath.

"I'm your bodyguard, Francesca. I can't just misplace you and forget about it."

"I'll come back before he does. He doesn't need to know. Please, Jamie." I back up a few steps and glance through the riverboat windows as I talk. Two waiters stride along the corridor inside, dressed in black jackets and white shirts.

Huh. I shift the phone so it's squeezed between my shoulder and ear and pull up the hem of my shirt dress. I tie it in a knot at my back at the waist of my leggings, as close to a shirt and black pants as I can make it look.

"It's not safe, Frankie." Jamie doesn't sound pissed anymore. He sounds scared. That on its own is almost enough for me to give it up—to tell him where to find me and limp back into his arms.

Almost. But not quite. I whip my head up and down the street, eyeing all the chairs scattered over the cafe sidewalks.

"I'm twenty-two. If I can't survive a week on my own, we can chalk it up to natural selection."

"Don't even *joke*—"

My phone buzzes against my cheek. I pull it down and flip it over in my palm, glancing at the screen.

Location services activated.

Really? That's how he wants to play it? Pleading and reasonable in my ear, at the same time as tracking my cell phone?

"Jamie?"

"Yes?" He sounds uneasy. He heard my phone buzz too.

"Do me a favor, okay? Go jump in the river."

I hang up, my thumb shaking, I'm so angry, and limp to the cafe tables. I've already spotted what I need, and thanks to Jamie, I no longer give a shit.

"Excuse me, sir." I bump into the back of a diner as he chats up another businessman. They're clustered around a shining metal table, shirt sleeves rolled and cigars puffing away like it's not 10am. Glass bottles of beer, sweating in the heat, rattle on the table as I jar it.

"Hey!" The men all glare and snap at me, then immediately turn guilty when they see my limp. I smile sweetly and hold up my traitorous cell phone, currently broadcasting my location to Jamie.

"This was on the ground right by your table. Did one of you guys drop this?"

They all pat their pockets, murmuring to each other, eyes glued on the phone.

It's a nice model. Expensive. Dad doesn't buy his daughter cheap crap. Gotta keep her entertained, I guess, when you lock her away for eight years.

"Oh, that must be mine!" The man nearest me smiles up at me, his cheeks dimpling. He's handsome, in that groomed sort of way. A plastic banker. He holds his palm out for the phone, eyes twinkling, and I drop it into his grip happily.

He thinks he's taking me for a ride. What an asshole. It's not like he needs the money.

He might need a doctor, though, once he's done explaining himself to Jamie.

"Thanks, darlin'."

I beam like he's the prettiest thing I've ever seen. "You're welcome!"

Then I turn and pretend to stumble, knocking over his bottle of beer. They all shoot out of their seats, cursing and trying to save their shirts and their cigars, and I whisk his black suit jacket off the back of his chair. I stride away, not bothering to apologize.

He shouldn't have claimed my phone.

It's not the best fit. The banker had fairly wide shoulders, and I have to roll his sleeves up past my wrists. But it's a black jacket and a white shirt, and when I stride up the walkway to the riverboat, nobody tries to stop me. I nod and smile at the man sitting in the ticket booth like I come to work here every day.

He blinks at me, confused, but raises his hand in a wave.

Then I limp up the ramp, over the waves sucking the dock walls, and step on board.

* * *

The floor tilts from side to side, the faint tinkling of piano drifting down the corridor. I can hear the clink of cutlery and the hum of conversation, but as I tuck myself beside the window and stare at the street outside, my pulse swells to fill my ears.

It doesn't take long. Less than five minutes. Then Jamie bursts out of the alley.

He's flushed, his suit jacket flapping as he runs, his phone held out in front of him. He glances down at the screen as he weaves between cafe tables and around strollers on the sidewalk.

I bite down hard on my lip as he slows to a walk. He frowns

down at his screen, then whips his head around. I jerk back against the corridor wall, plastering myself to the painted green wood.

My palms grow slick where they're pressed against the wall. I count to ten, slow and steady, then risk a peek back through the window.

Jamie holds the banker's collar in one fist, draping the man over the cafe table. He shakes him hard, rattling his head, then hammers his fist into the man's face. I wince, chewing the inside of my cheek. I've never seen Jamie in action. Not really.

It's easier to picture him firing that gun, now.

Jamie beats on the guy a couple more times, the other businessmen long gone. Red spots shine on the guy's white shirt, and his black jacket itches my neck.

It's messed up of me, but I'm still not sorry. Especially not when the guy points a shaking finger down the street. Jamie drops him like a stone and takes off, running in the direction he pointed.

Running away from the riverboat.

I press my fingers into the seam between boards on the wall. My breath fogs the glass as I watch Jamie's red hair disappear into the crowds. I let out a sigh, but nearly choke on my tongue when the boat lurches and rumbles to life. The buzz of the engine vibrates through the soles of my shoes, all the way to my teeth.

The ticket man drags the wooden ramp on board, locking the gate shut behind him.

He winks at me as he stows the ramp, tying it off with a wet, frayed rope.

"Better hop to it. You know how Gabriel gets about slackers."

I nod, forcing a shaky smile, and push away from the wall.

Hop to it. Yeah. I guess I work on the riverboat, now.

Chapter 3

From the soft strains of piano and the tinkle of cutlery, I figure this is a silver service kind of place. You know: cocktail dresses and tuxes, at least at night. Designer day dresses the rest of the time. I smooth myself down as best I can in the corridor, retying the knot of my shirt dress to make it sit flatter at my waistband.

I roll the jacket sleeves all the way to my elbow, and fasten a single button right between my breasts. There's nothing I can do about my bright yellow sneakers, nor my crazy, wind-tangled hair. I finger comb it, but it puffs up bigger with each run of my fingers until I give up altogether.

Show time.

I stroll down the corridor towards the hum of conversation, forcing myself to walk without a limp. It burns a little more, but at least this way I'll draw fewer eyes. I'm already fairly bedraggled for a waitress, after all, and thanks to my injury and Dad's efforts, I've never worked a day in my life.

All those times I begged to send out resumes; all those offers I made to shadow his workers. Those jobs would really have come in handy right about now.

Still: carrying food around and serving drinks. How hard can it be?

Two hours later, I have my answer: really damn hard.

"Table six is up, and they want new napkins." A server with short brown hair and freckles dusting the bridge of her nose jabs a finger at the food station.

"Again?" I ask, hurrying to the plates. They're so hot, they make me hiss and snatch my hand back.

"I know, right?" The girl rolls her eyes as she wraps rolls of cutlery at lightning speed. "You should offer their drinks in a sippy cup next time."

I'm pretty sure that's a joke, but if you ask me it's also a great idea. If grown-ass adults are going to spill every drink they're given, they should have plastic cups with handles.

I balance the plates on my forearm the way I've seen the other waiters do, but it takes me an age to shuffle to their table. The food's probably half cold by the time I set their plates down.

"And the napkins?" One of the diners slurs, bleary-eyed. Seriously, no wonder they spill everything.

"I'll fetch those for you right away, sir."

I make sure to dab one on my sweaty forehead before I bring it over.

By the third hour, I'm cursing all the terrible choices that brought me here. My leg screams with every step I take, and I'm taking thousands. The servers don't get a chance to breathe, let alone sit. I'm sweaty and crabby, I've been spilled on and cursed at, and this is a fancy place.

I don't want to know what it's like working in the bar everyone keeps mentioning. The one on the upper deck, with blues music and dancing and darts. Poker games and pool tables, and booze on tap all day long.

I don't know anyone's names, and they don't know mine, but they're all too rushed to care. I'm an extra pair of hands—who cares if I'm meant to be here? After all, what kind of idiot stowaway would sneak on board to work a shift?

A desperate one, that's who. I swipe my arm across my forehead and wrinkle my nose at the sticky, damp skin. Through the fogged up windows, the city skyline inches past, lit orange in the buttery afternoon sunshine. For the millionth time, I wonder where Jamie is.

How mad he is.

If he'll get in real trouble with Dad.

"Look alive."

I jump and hobble out of the way of a server pushing a stainless steel cart. It's loaded up and groaning with steaming plates and tureens of soup; bowls of collard greens and a basket of flaky bread rolls. My stomach clenches as the delicious scents waft up my nose.

When did I last eat? That damn banana, that's when.

The reality of my situation comes crashing down on my tired shoulders. I'm a stowaway on a riverboat. I've got no phone, no money, no ID. Once the boat docks again tonight, I've got nowhere to go but back home with my tail between my legs.

Back to Jamie's furious silence and to endless lectures from Dad over the phone.

Back to the same garden walls I've stared at a hundred times before. The same rooms, the same books, the same life.

My leg throbs, hot and pulsing, and I sniff back tears. I stumble blindly to the exit, ignoring the frustrated calls from the other servers. The room tilts, half from the river waves and half from my dizzy brain.

The deck. Fresh air. I just need to get my head on straight. I've stolen one week of freedom, and I'm going to enjoy every second, damn it.

My sneakers catch on the narrow stairs, but I grip the handrail tight and force myself up the steps. When I spill out on deck, the wind slaps my cheeks and lifts my hair. It's perfect: cool and calming, whispering over my clammy skin. All those panicked thoughts that were rising up my throat and threatening to choke me—they drift away, blown loose by the breeze.

I've been here longer than I thought. The day's light is dimming, the sun bleeding where it hits the horizon. It lights up the river silver, the moon and the first few stars dusting the sky, and the beauty of this moment wraps a hand around my heart and squeezes tight.

God damn.

I wish Jamie was here to see this.

My feet drag over the deck as I limp to the guardrail. It's ornate, the metal curling and swirling, and I run the tip of one finger along the back of a curl.

"Well, I know you're not the safety inspector."

I sniff hard and wrap my hand around the railing. When I lean over, my stomach swoops, but the churning water floats up in a mist and cools my cheek.

"Girlie. I'm talking to you."

I rock back on my heels and glance around. A man stands with his arms crossed over a barrel chest. His shirt is open at the collar—navy blue and worn, a worker's shirt—and dark chest hairs dust the light brown skin beneath. He's huge, well over six feet and broad with it too.

The sort of man my dad would hire to... persuade people. Back in the day.

Except there's silver threaded through the black hair at this man's temples and speckled through his short beard. Fine lines crease his dark eyes.

"Me?" I croak, pointing my thumb at myself like an idiot. I glance around, but there's no one else near. I'm alone in the shadows on the deck of a riverboat, tucked away with a strange man.

A man whose lips are curved down in a frown. Whose eyes glitter as he watches me.

"Who else?" His voice is low and gravelly. I shrug and wrap my arms around myself, cinching my stolen jacket tighter.

He waits for me to say something. To explain myself, I guess. But something tells me he'd never believe me if I tried, and even if he did... well, no man in this city is foolish enough to piss off Carrick O'Brien.

When it becomes clear that I'm done talking, the man's frown deepens. He steps closer, his arms unfolding and his thumbs hooking in his jeans pockets.

"I know you're not on my staff."

My eyebrows shoot up my forehead. "You're in charge?"

He glowers at me, but I can't help my surprise. He doesn't exactly look like a man who'd run a fancy riverboat cruise. He looks more like he should be in an old-timey engine room, shoveling coal into a giant burner.

"Answer me this." The man steps closer again and rests a palm on the rail. I glance down, my eyes snagging on the blunt knuckles of his worn hands. They look like hands with calluses. Scars. Hands that tell their owners' story. "Why does a little rich girl sneak onto a boat without paying, then play at being a waitress all day?"

"How did you..." I clear my throat. "What makes you think I'm rich?" I turn the pockets of the banker's jacket inside out, and a receipt for a fancy restaurant flutters to my feet. "Um.

That's not mine."

The man snorts. "Yeah, no shit."

I raise my chin and go for broke. What do I have to lose? If this guy were a psycho, he could have tipped me overboard by now. Worst-case scenario—he calls the cops when he drops me back at the docks.

That won't be a problem. Carrick O'Brien has friends in all sorts of places.

"I'm auditioning. I want a job."

The man tilts his head, the ghost of a smile tugging at his lips. He's got a wide mouth, but it looks good on him. It's a mouth that makes your mind wander.

"Oh yeah? You going to walk off in the middle of your paid shifts, too?"

"If I need air, sure."

"You haven't worked much, have you?"

I grin and shrug. "This might be my first day."

The man smirks and rocks forward, his chest swaying an inch closer to mine, then settles back on his heels. I scrape the toe of my sneaker over the deck, heart pounding in my chest.

Jesus, I'm so freaking nervous. I haven't felt this jangled up since middle school. I tuck my hair behind my ear and firm up my shoulders, forcing myself to stand up straight.

I'm a grown woman. An adult. And a worker too, if I have any say in it.

"All right." My mouth drops open, but he keeps going, saying the most beautiful things I've ever heard. "Are you a day worker, stowaway, or are you looking for room and board, too?"

"Yes." I lick my lips. I can't believe my freaking luck. Someone up there behind those stained pink clouds is watching over me. "Room. Board. That one, please."

"I'll take it out of your wages." He winks at me, and I near enough wilt over the railing. "Go and find Michelle. She'll sort your uniform and lodging. Then be in the top bar in twenty minutes."

"What about a break?" I call after his back. He spins around, still walking backwards, and lifts his palms.

"Why would you need a break, stowaway? You haven't started your shift yet."

Damn it. I give him a thumbs up, then flip him off when he turns back around.

Fine. I test my weight on my leg and wince. I need painkillers, stat.

Painkillers, a big jug of water, and a basket of those dinner rolls. I'm about to start my first job.

Working for the sexiest man I think I've ever seen.

Jesus Christ.

* * *

"Make it again." The head bartender slams a pint glass down on the bar, barely an inch from my finger. I blink at him, then frown at the beer I just poured.

Maybe a third of the glass is honey-colored liquid. The rest is slowly collapsing foam.

"All right." I pull a fresh glass off the shelf and limp to the right pump. I gave up on forcing myself to walk normally after an hour. I figure I've got bigger issues.

Like how the hell you pour a damn beer, for one. It looks so easy when everyone else does it. I glare at the tap, tilting the glass like I was shown, pulling steadily on the handle.

The tap splutters and hisses, then explodes foam all over

the bar. I let go of the handle, plonking the glass down and stepping back with my hands held up.

Maybe it's for the best that Dad never let me work. I'm a walking disaster.

First the beer taps. Then that tiny spill with the fresh keg. Then the jar of peanuts I knocked onto the floor. Since I set foot in the top deck bar, I've left a trail of destruction.

Across the room, bent over a laptop in a booth, the owner flicks his eyes up to me. I swipe a cloth over my splattered black t-shirt.

Every crash, every spill, every yelp when I step on the head bartender Harley's foot. Dark eyes flick up to me, each time getting narrower and narrower.

I'm screwing this up. I'm screwing this up so bad.

"I'm sorry," I say again, scrubbing at the puddles of foam on the bar then dabbing at Harley's narrow chest. He flaps me away, his jaw tight as he turns to serve another customer.

"Miss?" A soft voice calls down the bar. I turn to find a handsome man leaning on his elbows. He's got smooth dark skin and tight black curls, and a dusting of stubble over his jaw.

His eyes crinkle at me when he smiles, and I let out a gust of air.

"Sure. Well, brace yourself."

He chuckles as I limp down the bar to take his order. His eyes track to my leg but they don't linger there, shooting straight back up to my face.

I wait for the pity. The twisted mouth, the sympathetic grimace.

It doesn't come. He just smiles, his face pure sunshine, and asks for a glass of water.

Water. All right. Even I've poured some waters in my day.

Since this is the first drink I haven't screwed up in a while, I really go ham on it. I give him ice, and two slices of lime, and place it on the bar on a square paper napkin.

"Beautifully done."

I drop a curtsy. "Why, thank you."

I'm not sure if we're supposed to charge for waters, but I figure it's a human right or something. It should be free.

Hot Boss can always dock the lime slices from my wages. It's not like I'm here to make a quick buck.

"You come here often?" I ask, grabbing another glass and polishing it with my cloth. I'm pretty sure it achieves exactly nothing, but it looks cool. Like in the movies.

The guy smiles wider. "Isn't that my line?"

I cock my head, frowning. "Are you saying you don't think I've worked here long?"

His soft laughter is a balm to my nerves. My heart's been hammering like a jackrabbit all day, and especially since the owner cornered me on deck. I like to think that's why I've been so clumsy this first shift, but who knows? Maybe I am that useless.

"I would have seen you, that's all."

I take him in again. His pressed green shirt, sleeves buttoned at the wrist. His water order.

"You're on the staff?"

He dips his chin. "Pianist."

Huh. There's a piano in this room, same as the restaurant downstairs, but it's shadowed in the corner right now. There's a guitarist propped on a stool instead, sweating under a spotlight and plucking out tunes.

"Are you gonna play in here?"

"Sure." He twinkles at me. "You gonna listen?"

I shrug, flicking my cloth over my shoulder. "Depends how loud I am dropping stuff."

He throws back his head and laughs, the sound rich and warm, and over his shoulder Hot Boss's eyes flick to me again.

Busted. I push away from the bar and limp back to a glowering Harley.

"Keep me in mind for your water needs," I call over my shoulder. The pianist nods and raises his glass, toasting me as I walk away.

"You managed to pour one drink," Harley says stiffly as I join him by the register. "It's a relief, but let's not get carried away."

I poke my tongue out at his back when he bends to open the fridge, but when he straightens again I'm smiling, sweet as pie.

"Sort these out. Restock any that are running low. Keep the labels facing front. Can you handle that?"

I nod and give him two thumbs up.

"Sort. Restock. Labels. Got it."

I crack my head against the bar as I lower myself to my knees. Harley mutters to himself as he walks away.

* * *

I've heard maestros and world famous musicians. Back when he let me out, Dad took me to music halls in the city, and once even to Carnegie Hall. I love music, same way as I love dance.

I've never heard someone play the piano like this. Kingston—that's the pianist's name, according to my crabby fellow bartender—dances his fingers over the keys, swaying on his stool like he's playing with his whole body. His eyes have drifted shut, his face peaceful, and the sounds he coaxes out of that instrument are unearthly. They ache.

"Good, isn't he?"

I jerk up from where I'm folded over the bar. The man from the deck stands in a patch of shadow, his thumbs hooked in his pockets. He watches Kingston, his shoulders relaxed, and I'm only half sure he's talking to me at all.

"Uh. Yeah, I'll say. He sounds like a damn angel."

The boss's mouth quirks to the side.

"A damn angel? That's a trick."

I snatch a cloth up and scrub at old scuff marks on the bar.

"Yeah, well. You asked."

Is it normal for a boss to come and chat with the staff? It's freaking nerve-wrecking. My hands tremble as I lever the dishwasher open and a cloud of steam hits my face. I set to putting the glasses back on their shelves, trying my best to ignore the man watching my every move.

"You really haven't worked before, have you?"

Harley snorts from where he's stood over the register, reading through a long receipt.

"Nope," I tell the cocktail glass in my hand. I grab a cloth and wipe away a tiny smear on the rim. "I told you. First day."

The man sighs and drums on the bar, then drops his hand.

"All right, then. Come with me, Frankie."

I'd be a fool not to notice Harley's smirk, or the grave set of the boss's mouth. I place my cloth and glass down, heart sinking to my gut, and walk out from behind the bar.

I don't limp. I make sure to measure each step, and raise my chin high. I may be a shitty bartender, but I have my pride.

Still, pride or no, I thank the heavens when the boss leads me to a door just a ways down the corridor. It's a little grander than the other doors, though not by much, and has a frosted glass pane set into the wood. I peer over the boss's shoulder as he slides the key into the lock, trying to make out the dark shapes behind the glass.

Gabriel Ortiz, the bronze plaque on the door says.

"Are you Gabriel?" I ask as the door swings open. The boss waves me inside.

"What gave me away?"

The office is small but refined. It's all dark, polished woods and bronze drawer handles. The porthole is bigger than the rest of the boat—big enough to see the city lights; the stars and the silvery waves—and deep blue velvet curtains hang on either side. Standing lamps cast warm pools of light, and stacks of paper on the desk are pinned in place by cloudy glass paperweights.

Gabriel gestures for me to sit, then lowers himself behind the desk.

"Frankie." He leans his elbows on the wood and steeples his fingers. I try not to stare outright at his hands again—I'm going to get a reputation. "Let's talk. You sneak onto my boat without a thing in your possession. You talk your way into a job you clearly cannot do. You know no one here. You have no skills."

I wince at each new point on his list, shrinking down in my chair.

"I won't alert the police to your presence, but you can't hide away on my boat. Whatever this is, I won't be involved. When we dock again tonight, I want you gone. Do you understand?"

I lick my lips, heart thundering.

"I'm not a criminal."

Gabriel tilts his head. His dark eyes glitter as they roam over my face.

"Then why are you here?"

I reach for the right words. For the perfect thing to say which will make this stranger trust me with his boat, his staff, his reputation.

They don't exist.

I sigh and slump down until my chin hovers an inch above my collarbone.

"I just wanted to get away."

"From?" Gabriel prompts.

"From my life. Just for a few days. I wanted to see what it would be like: working, meeting people. You know, doing normal stuff."

Gabriel pinches the bridge of his nose. "This isn't a holiday camp for rich girls."

"I know that. I can be helpful. I'll work for free."

"It's not free when you break so many glasses, Frankie."

I blow out a breath and tilt back on my chair, staring up at the ceiling. If I close my eyes, I can imagine I'm seeing straight through all this metal and wood, all the way up to the stars.

At least I spent the day on a boat. I heard Kingston play piano. I pissed off Harley. It wasn't a total waste.

When my chair legs thump back down on the floorboards, Gabriel watches me with a slight frown.

"I'll clear out when we dock." I shove my chair back and stand, suddenly ready to be gone. "Pleasure to meet you, Gabriel Ortiz. Thanks for today."

He hesitates, then clasps my hand in his own. His grip dwarfs mine, his palm warm and dry, and I linger just for a second to feel the thrum of his pulse under my fingertips.

I squeeze and let go. Gabriel watches me, face unreadable, even when I give him my jauntiest salute.

"See you around, Boss Man."

I hide my limp all the way to the hall, then collapse back against the closed door. Where the hell are my clothes, again?

I take a deep breath, count to ten, and head into the warren.

* * *

"You're going already?"

The girl from the restaurant with the short brown hair and freckles frowns down at me from the top bunk. I shrug and turn my back, pulling the bar's black t-shirt over my head and tossing it onto the bottom bunk.

This narrow bed was nearly mine. This girl, Tessa, was nearly my bunk mate. I was so damn close.

Shame I can't pour a drink to save my life. For the thousandth time today, I curse my dad for not letting me work.

"Not up to scratch. It's fine. I've got plenty of places to go," I lie.

The inky darkness outside the porthole looks vast. Endless. The city lights are bigger now, drifting closer as we come in to dock. I won't miss the lurching floor, at least, or the constant vibration through the soles of my feet.

"Damn. Gabriel hardly ever fires people. He must really not like you."

I duck my head to snatch up my white shirt dress, hiding how much that stings. I don't know why—I've known this man for all of an afternoon—but something about him makes me crave his approval.

I guess the doctor may be right about me needing therapy.

A sharp knock sounds at the door, and it pushes open before I can reply. Gabriel stands in the doorway, his eyes tracking over my bra and bare stomach.

His gaze flicks up to mine and stays there. My core throbs hot in my leggings.

"Give us a minute, Tessa."

His voice is so low and quiet, you could have missed it. But something tells me that Gabriel Ortiz never has to repeat himself. Tessa sits up and shimmies down the ladder to her bunk, raising her eyebrow at me before darting out of the room.

I remember I'm standing there gawping in just a bra, and throw my shirt dress over my head. It's tangled up, one of the sleeves inside out, and I thrash around as I get all mixed up and jumbled.

"Here." Steady hands pull my shirt so it's the right way round and settle it over my head. I blink at Gabriel as he turns my sleeve right-side-out, and taps me on the shoulder to keep dressing.

"Thanks," I mumble, sliding an arm into a sleeve. This isn't exactly helping my case that I could be a good worker. I can't even put my damn shirt on when a handsome man flusters me.

"We're docking in ten minutes."

Right. He's here to escort me off the boat. I puff up my chest, all ready to be offended, then remember I snuck onboard without paying in the first place.

I deflate like a popped balloon.

"All right. I'm ready to go." I snatch up my stolen jacket—more evidence of my untrustworthy ways—and slide it on over my shirt.

Gabriel doesn't move. He stays rooted to the spot, gazing at me with his mouth turned down.

It's an effort to keep the snap out of my voice.

"I'm not going to cause any trouble." Then, for good measure, I point at my crumpled uniform on the bed. "That's the only mess I'm leaving behind, I swear."

"That, and three trash cans of broken glass."

I huff. "Take it out of my wages."

"I haven't paid you anything."

"Exactly."

This is fun and all—no straight woman with a pulse wouldn't enjoy being shut in a small room with Gabriel Ortiz. He's got that grumpy, smouldering vibe down pat, and this close I can smell him, too. He smells like the fresh salty breeze up on deck.

It's time to go, though. Now I know I'm not wanted here, I'm counting down the seconds until I set foot back on land.

I'm not worried about being on the docks alone at night. It's not like I'll have to do much to get Jamie's attention. He's probably got an entire network of eyes, watching for me all over the city. And if he's told Dad I'm missing already—well, let's just say I'm surprised there aren't divers scaling the riverboat hull.

"Wait." A hand shoots out and grabs my shoulder as I head for the door. He's not gripping me hard, but something about that hand on me makes me sway on the spot. The warmth of his palm bleeds through my jacket and shirt, and spreads over my skin.

I mean… what the hell, right? I'm never going to see Gabriel Ortiz again. And who knows when I'll next be alone with a man who's not Jamie or my father.

I spin on my heel and throw my arms around Gabriel's neck. I have to push up onto my toes to do it, plastering my body against his chest. His eyes widen and he stumbles back, hands falling automatically to my waist.

"Ever make out with someone you just fired?"

Gabriel looks choked. "You're half my age."

"Kind of sexy, right?"

He's so close, his lips mere inches from mine, but I'm at my full height. Short of climbing him like a monkey, he's going to have to meet me partway.

Gabriel lets out a shaky breath, his grip tightening on my waist. My heart thuds faster and I tilt my face up, my eyes drifting closed.

Firm hands push me back on my heels, and Gabriel steps away.

"You're not fired. I came to say you can stay."

I chew on my bottom lip. I came here to experience life. To have an adventure. Sure, that could mean working the top deck bar.

Or it could mean kissing the stern, muscled boss.

I step closer. "You won't kiss a staff member?" Gabriel shakes his head wordlessly. "If I turn down the job, will you kiss me then?"

He shuts his eyes like I'm physically paining him, holding out a hand to stop me coming further forward.

"You wanted to stay and work. So stay and work." He opens his eyes, and they burn into me in the dim cabin. "But the first sign of trouble and you're gone. You understand?"

I nod and wrap my arms around my waist as I watch him duck back out the narrow doorway.

A normal person would probably be ashamed right now. Horrifically embarrassed. But I figure I've probably got a day or two tops before Jamie catches up to me here.

I'm like one of those fireflies who lives for a day. No time to be shy.

It's time to be bold.

Chapter 4

Back on the estate, I can sleep in as late as I like. I rarely rise before the sun's up and shining, and Jamie's come knocking on my bedroom door with a steaming mug of coffee in his hand.

I never thought of it as lazy. What was there to get up for, really? But now, tumbling out of my bunk just past dawn, Past Frankie is like a distant memory. That girl had it comfortable, all right.

Comfortable, but stifling.

My bunk mate Tessa is not a morning person. She hits the floor with a grunt, and barely strings three syllables together for the whole time we're getting ready. There are showers down the hall—tiny cubicles that spray boiling hot, then icy cold—and I find a pile of fresh clothes in the hall outside our door.

Uniform t-shirts and stretchy black pants. All my size.

Underwear would have been handy, too, but I guess Gabriel has to draw the line somewhere. I settle for going commando and hope my pants aren't too thin.

"Is the boss like your sugar daddy or something?" Tessa eyes the pile of clothes with distrust when I squeeze back through the doorway after my shower. My wet hair is cold already, dripping icy water onto my towel.

I snort, tossing the pile of clothes on my unmade bed. "I wish."

Tess grins—the first real sign of life since she woke up. "I hear that. There's something about a stern older man."

I press my palms together and pray up to the ceiling. "Amen."

Apparently perving over your boss is as good a bonding experience as any, because Tessa crooks her arm through mine as we head up to the main deck. All around us, fellow workers spill out of doorways and stumble down the halls, blinking the night's sleep from their eyes.

There's no sign of Gabriel. But I guess he doesn't sleep mixed in with the flock.

I concentrate on walking properly as we go. I don't want to draw attention, not yet. And if people think I'm not up to the job, they won't want to work with me.

I've got who knows how many more hours of freedom. I don't want to spend them pissing folk off.

We gather on deck like a horde of uniformed zombies, the breeze smacking our cheeks awake. I draw a big breath into my lungs, picking out the scent of freshwater and river weed. There's cinnamon, too, floating up from the kitchens, and the tang of soap from everyone's showers.

"All right," Gabriel calls from the front of the deck. He doesn't shout. He doesn't need to. Everyone falls silent, their mouths snapping shut, and we all stare at him as one.

It must be weird, commanding that kind of attention. Kind of stressful, too.

"You know the drill. Split into your teams and finish up your areas before doors open." Through the crowd, Gabriel's eyes fall on me, and I shift on the spot. I can't look away; I stare at him, hypnotized. Does he have this effect on everyone?

Tessa nudges me, and I tear my eyes away from Gabriel to glance over at her. She's smirking, her face turned straight ahead.

Damn it.

Gabriel calls out more announcements, but he might as well be speaking Pig Latin for all the good it does me. I don't know what the different parts of the boat are called; I don't recognize half these tasks. It drills into me again just how little I know about the world beyond my father's estate walls.

My chest throbs, and I glance out over the docks. We came back last night after midnight, letting off the passengers and tying up for the night. The whole time, I was waiting for Jamie to rush on board and drag me out by my ear.

Half of me was even hoping for it. Isn't that insane? It's not that I want to go home just yet, but this is the longest I've been away from Jamie for years.

I miss him. I wish I could tell him about all this stuff.

But the second he knows where I am, he'll drag me straight home. And he must be so spitting mad by now, he'll probably never speak to me again.

The docks are bustling this time of the morning. Cafe owners sweep the cobblestones and set out their tables and chairs. White gulls and pigeons flutter down to the stone, picking for scraps and crumbs. And men in overalls with garbage pickers stroll up and down, picking up the remains of the parade.

Feathers and beads. Food wrappers and beer cans. The city partied hard last night.

"You stay with Tessa." Gabriel's voice makes me jump; he's stood square in front of me. Everyone else mills away, off to their allotted tasks.

"Sure," I rasp after clearing my throat. The man looks tired. The lines around his eyes are deep, and I fight the urge to smooth out his creased forehead with my fingertip.

He looks for a second like he's going to say something. He lingers, chewing the inside of his cheek. Then someone calls for him across the deck, and he's off, striding away.

"Girl." Tessa gives me the side eye. I blow out a breath.

"I know."

It's a relief to duck back inside, the shadows cloaking the flush on my cheeks.

* * *

We're assigned to clean up the top deck bar, on account of how I personally made half the mess. It's Tessa, the pianist Kingston and I, and Tessa sets the radio blaring.

"No need to clean without music," she calls from over by the pool tables. "This ain't prison."

Back home, we have a staff of cleaners, vetted to high heaven by Jamie. I try to pick up after myself—I'm not an asshole, you know—but it's been a long time since I was acquainted with a sponge. Tessa throws her head back and cackles when she sees me pinching one between finger and thumb.

"Wear gloves, you damn fool. Are you on day release from private school?"

"I'm in college," I sniff, tugging on gloves. I'm no teenage school girl.

"That's even worse," she hoots, dragging a mop and bucket out from behind the bar. She has a point, so I shut my trap and set to scrubbing down the fridges. It's a clean boat with high standards, but even so it's nasty work. I wrinkle my nose so much for the first hour, it's in danger of setting like that.

Still, I kind of like it after a while. My muscles burn like they haven't in months, and Tessa and Kingston don't go easy on me. They give me my fair share of the work, and they expect me to keep up, leg be damned.

I do, too. I keep up just fine, especially after I stop forcing myself to walk normally. I limp my merry way around the bar, cleaning up in time to the music like a mouse in a Disney movie.

For a crazy second, I let myself picture it: staying here. Working a job.

Then Dad's face floats before my eyes, and I slam right back to earth.

Day release isn't far from the truth. Tessa's closer than she knows.

The song changes on the radio, turning from something poppy and upbeat to something slower and pulsing. Something gooey. Kingston whoops and grabs the mop from Tessa, twirling the handle around as he sways and dances the blues.

His hips sway. His knees pulse. Kingston's liquid gold, spreading out over the tiles.

Hot damn, he's a mover.

I drop my sponge on the bar and tug my gloves off. The sun spills through the round windows, casting golden slants of light over the bar floorboards, dust motes spinning in the air. I grin as I cross to Kingston, adding an extra spring to my step.

"Save a dance for me after the mop."

He turns, surprised, his eyes dropping to my leg, but there's no pity or scorn on his face when he smiles and drops the wooden handle. The mop clatters to the floor, splattering soapy water. Kingston holds out a palm.

"You a dancer, Frankie?"

I shrug, limping closer. "One of the all-time greats."

All right, I'm not that, but I'm not half bad either, never mind my leg. I've had lessons at the estate for years, even before the injury. Dad is a romantic at heart, and he insisted Tommy and I both learn to dance.

There's no better way to frighten a man, he told me once, winking as he spun me around the front deck. The sun was bleeding into the horizon, and the scent of jasmine drifted on the breeze. *Dance with his wife, sweep her off her feet, and he'll be putty in your hands.*

I've never swept any wives away, but I'm ready to take a crack at Kingston.

Blues dancing is slow and close. Legs slotted and hands held. Drifting over the floor together like a lazy summer breeze. And Kingston can dance almost as well as he plays piano, his lead sure and his steps precise. He finds little pockets inside the music—hidden rhythms—and we dance to those too, mining the song for all it's got.

I can't do every step exactly right—not without twinging my leg. But I alter the steps, keeping time, and we more than make do.

"Jeez Louise." I blow my hair out of my face as the song croons to an end. Kingston smiles down at me, his brown eyes crinkling. "And I thought it was hot in here before."

He leans close, his lips grazing the shell of my ear as he spins us around on the spot, the next song starting right up.

"I bet every room's scorching when you walk in, Frankie."

I snort at his collarbone. "Yeah, the guys love the limp."

Kingston shrugs, his shoulders loose.

"I call it like I see it."

I bite my lips to hold back my grin.

"Done already?" The sound of Gabriel's voice has us leaping apart. I land funny on my leg and stumble, wincing, and his eyes track straight to me.

I wipe my face clean. No pain, no guilt. A few feet away, Gabriel watches me, a muscle ticking in his jaw.

"We're all set," Kingston tells him, all sunshine and light.

Gabriel nods once, sharp, and says: "A word."

I leave them to it, glancing over my shoulder as I limp back to the bar. My leg's hot and aching, telling me off for daring to dance a whole song.

It was worth it. I haven't danced like that in years: so absorbed in the song, you forget time's passing. You forget everything except the rhythm and your partner's hold.

There's a wobbly stool with a faded red leather seat, and I drag it out behind the register. I plop myself down and drag over the basket of bread rolls Tessa swiped from the kitchen for breakfast.

Flaky. Crisp on the outside, but soft and warm in the middle. It's all I can do to stop my eyes rolling back in my head.

The phone rings, interrupting my intimate moment with the bread. I glance around the bar, but Tessa's scrubbing the far windows, and Gabriel and Kingston are locked in an intense conversation. They murmur to each other, gesturing and squaring up. Hoo, boy.

I slide the ringing phone off its hook and press it to my ear.

"Good morning, this is…" My brain stutters, and I can't for the life of me remember the name of the boat. Did I ever read it? Am I going insane? "… This is the best darn riverboat in town. How may I help you?"

"Frankie?" Jamie's voice is rough. Urgent. I slam the phone

down without thinking, my pulse thundering in my ears. Guess he found me.

Everything I should have done comes to me in a rush. I should have used a fake name; should have stayed away from the phone; should have left first thing this morning and squeaked out another day's adventure.

But then I'd have missed my dance with Kingston. I draw a cardboard straw out of a glass jar and gnaw on the end.

Fifteen minutes until we set sail, give or take, according to the clock above the pool tables. There's no way Jamie will miss that deadline. That leaves fifteen minutes to hurry back onto the street and lose him again in the city.

Or… the thought curls my lips into an evil smirk.

Fifteen minutes to evade Jamie on board… then an entire day together on the riverboat.

I'm doing him a favor, really. Jamie is the only person in the world who needs to get out more than me. He's always so stressed, running the estate security. Doing God-knows-what for Dad and the business.

Yes. A day on the river is exactly what Jamie needs.

* * *

I don't run. Or limp, or skip, or hustle. I sit on my stool and chew on my straw, and practice what I'm going to say to Jamie.

Of course, I can't be too easy to find. Too easy, and he'll drag me straight back onto the dock. And he'll locate my cabin in two seconds flat.

"Do a girl a favor?"

I grin at Kingston as I cross the bar floorboards, breaking up his murmured argument with Gabriel. The boss of the boat turns to me too, rolling his eyes in exasperation.

That's fine. Now that Jamie's onto me, I won't be able to work here any longer. Gabriel Ortiz can think what he likes of me, and I can think what I like of him.

For starters: I think he looks delicious this morning.

"What's up, sweetheart?"

Normally a guy calling me sweetheart would get my hackles up. But Kingston says it like he actually means it, his face open and his smile bright, and I can't find it in myself to mind.

"I've been rumbled. Can I hide in your cabin for fifteen minutes? Just until we leave the dock."

Kingston's eyebrows shoot up as Gabriel glowers. He nods, opening his mouth to agree, but Gabriel cuts across him.

"I told you already: the first sign of trouble and you're gone. I'm not harboring any criminals, girl, not even ones who look like you."

"It's not the cops I'm hiding from." I take hold of Kingston's sleeve and tug him towards the door. "It's nothing illegal, I promise."

Gabriel crosses his arms and watches us back away, looking half ready to snatch me up and bundle me out through a porthole.

"Who are you hiding from?" he calls.

"My bodyguard!" I yell, just as we reach the doorway. I give him a thumbs up and drag Kingston out of the bar before anyone can ask more questions. Kingston keeps his lips sealed, too, all the way to his cabin where he tucks me onto the top bunk.

"Duck your head under the blankets if anyone comes in. That's the best I can do."

It's fair. It's not like there's a big closet to hide inside, or space under the bunks. The staff cabins are small and efficient, every spare inch used for storage.

Kingston tugs the blankets up to my shoulder, winking at me as he tucks them under my chin. Then he lingers, shifting on the spot, the question burning the tip of his tongue.

"Why do I need a bodyguard?" I supply for him. Kingston nods, relieved. "Because my father is Carrick O'Brien."

I watch his dark skin pale a few shades, and suddenly I want him gone. I don't want Kingston dragged into this at all if I can help it. Not if the very mention of my father clouds his eyes with fear like that.

"Better get back to work." He nods, biting his lip, but he still doesn't move. He looks scared for me. I fish a hand out of the blankets and stroke a fingertip down his cheek, marveling at how this gentle pianist wants to protect me.

"I'm not in any danger, I swear. I just wanted some time on my own. Jamie—my bodyguard—he'll be pissed, that's for sure, but he'd never hurt me."

"All right," Kingston rasps. "Well, you know where I am if you need me."

I nod and smile, my hair sliding over his pillow. It smells like him: like soap and basil. He reaches up and mirrors what I just did, stroking a fingertip down my cheek. I forget to breathe for a second, heart hammering in my chest, and when he turns away, I squirm under the covers.

Jeez. You'd think I spent the last eight years in a convent, not my family estate.

I guess in a way, I did, though a few of the gardener's boys might disagree.

* * *

The engines start up, rattling everything from the bedposts to my bones. I shuffle up the mattress and stare out the porthole, the glass fogging over from my breath. Outside, the dock slides past, and we turn away from the city. If I strain, I can hear the slosh of waves against the side of the boat.

Sorry, Jamie. This round goes to me.

He's going to be so damn angry with me, but I still can't help the grin stretching my cheeks. I fumble down the ladder, gripping tight to the metal bars, and hop down onto the floor of Kingston's cabin.

A sneaky little voice whispers in my brain, telling me to poke through Kingston's things. To see what he keeps in his drawers; to see what he wears off duty.

I shut that voice right up and cross to the door. I won't repay a man's kindness by violating his privacy, no matter the mean little thoughts in my head. After the 'accident', Dad and Jamie installed extra cameras all over the estate. Not just at the entrances and exits any more, but through the gardens and inside the rooms.

I know as well as anyone how badly we need a space of our own.

There's a slim chance Jamie didn't make it to the boat. That he didn't recognize my voice on the phone. That I have another full day before I'm made to face the music.

That hope dies a quiet death as I walk down the corridor to the bar. Raised voices echo in the cavernous room ahead, and I'd know him anywhere.

Jamie.

Something crashes against the bar and there's the tinkle of shattering glass. I speed up, bursting through the door and gaping at the scene before me.

Kingston slumps against the bar, his bottom lip cut. Jamie and Gabriel square up to each other, chests heaving and hands fisted. Gabriel is a few inches taller and broader, but Jamie is young, quick and angry. His suit jacket is creased, his white shirt splattered with blood drops, and he surges forward just as I step in the room.

"Hey!" I yell as loud as my lungs will let me. "Get off of them, Jamie!"

He spins, eyes wide and the fight forgotten, just as Gabriel swings for his cheek. Jamie crumples to the ground, head bouncing off the floorboards, and I cry out as I limp over.

"Was that necessary?" I spit at Gabriel, dropping to my knees next to my bodyguard. I pull his head into my lap, feeling for his pulse even though I wouldn't have a clue what to do if I didn't find one.

Gabriel stares between me and Jamie's passed out form, his chest still heaving. But when he points at me, his finger is steady.

"You've brought me nothing but trouble, girl. Keep quiet and away from me today, both of you, and don't you ever set foot on this boat after tonight."

I shut my mouth with a click, and he turns away. He sees to Kingston, checking on the younger man before clapping him on the shoulder and heading out the bar without another word.

"Sorry, Frankie." Kingston offers me a rueful smile, wincing as it stretches his hurt lip. The sight makes my heart sink right to my toes, and I feel about three inches tall.

Was a day on my own really worth all of this trouble?

"Since you can't come here again..." Kingston fishes a flyer from his back pocket and hands it to me. It's for a gig in the city tomorrow night—a blues bar. I fold it carefully and realize I don't have pockets, then glance around before tucking it into my bra.

"I'll try to come," I mumble, and Kingston chuckles.

"There's ice behind the bar for your man."

Jamie's not my man, not in the way he said it, but Kingston leaves before I can splutter my denials. Jamie groans in my lap, his eyelids fluttering, and I cradle his face, stroking his cheekbones with my thumbs.

He'll probably never speak to me after this. He'll get Dad to assign someone else to watch me. I card my fingers through his red hair, surprised at how soft it feels.

"I'm sorry," I whisper, twining a lock around my finger. "Please don't hate me for too long."

* * *

The sun crashes into the horizon by the time Jamie's ready to speak to me again. We sit on the deck, our sides pressed together on a bench for warmth against the slicing cold breeze, two mugs of coffee clutched in our hands. Crimson blooms across the sky, glinting off the gunmetal gray river.

"I'm sorry," I say for the hundredth time.

Jamie grunts, raising his mug to his mouth. His bottom lip is split, and a mottled bruise already darkens one eye. While I've been enjoying my little vacation from my life, Jamie looks like he's been fighting his way through a hedge backwards.

Guilt sloshes in my stomach, but there's something else, too. A pulse of defiance.

I'm sorry to give him a hard time, but I'm not sorry for wanting time to myself. I'm a grown woman, for God's sake, and I was hurt over eight years ago.

This can't be my whole existence. Bodyguards and cameras and walls. It just can't.

"Look." I blow out a harsh breath. "I know this has sucked for you. But I'll take the blame with Dad, and—"

"I haven't told him." Jamie's mouth twists as he stares out at the waves.

"You... really?" I lick my lips. "Well, that's perfect! He never needs to know."

Jamie turns to me, his face stony.

"Of course he does. I failed him. Failed you. Anything could have happened to you over the last two days. I'll tell him in person as soon as he's home, and that'll be that." Jamie sighs and turns back to the river, rubbing his thumb over the rim of his mug. "If he tosses me out on my ear, I'll be lucky."

"He won't do that." I swallow. "He wouldn't."

Jamie is family. He's been with us since I was a kid, and he was a gawky teenager. His parents got tangled up in some nasty business, and Dad took Jamie on when it was all over.

"I'm not Tommy," is all Jamie says. Well yeah, he's not wrong. Jamie is a thousand times better than my flesh and blood brother. Tommy barely knows I exist, and he treats our parents like a bank account—nothing more.

"Just as well," I mutter, and triumph flares in my chest when Jamie's cheeks flush pink. No, I don't want him to be my brother at all.

I push my luck, shuffling closer until we're sealed tight at the arm. Molded together. I hook my pinkie finger through his, and my heart sings. The city lights twinkle, and the stars throb overhead, and it's almost a perfect moment.

Almost, but not quite. Jamie slides away, putting three inches of cold air between us. I draw my hand back, trying not to feel too much like I've been kicked in the gut.

"He won't trust you after this. They'll make the doctor do home visits."

I'll never see the city again. It's a prison sentence, and the fact they can't see that makes me want to tear my hair out and scream.

"If he locks me up, he's worse than the men who hurt me. And if you help him, you are too."

Jamie splutters and looks at me, eyes wide, like he'd never thought of it as hurting me before. Oh sure, they can say it's for my protection, but I've had a taste of life now.

My existence on that estate is a shadow of what life can be.

I stand and place the mug on the bench, then leave him there as I wander to the rail. Flecks of water drift up from the waves, churned up by the breeze, and I sigh as they settle cool on my cheeks.

I'm ready to leave this boat. To step back on land.

But I won't go quietly back into my cage.

Chapter 5

Five days until my parents return.

Five days left with Jamie.

I yawn and stretch in my soft bed, so comfy after that hard, narrow bunk. I came home without a fight; went to bed without complaint. Even suggested Jamie join me, then chuckled at his blush.

Know when to fight and when to fold. Dad taught me that.

I spend the morning in strategy mode, going through the motions to keep Jamie happy. I rise late and take a long soak in the bath, moaning as the hot water soothes my aching leg. I scrub myself clean and dress in a crop top and yoga pants, moving through stretches on my bedroom floor.

Jamie pokes his head around the door more than he used to. His frown doesn't smooth out when he sees me each time, either. He nods and strides away before I can say anything, back to whatever brooding bodyguards do.

That's right. I'm just soaking and stretching. Nothing to see here.

As soon as he's gone, I dig my notebook out from under my cushions and scribble more notes. Places I want to go. Things I want to see and do. Ideas for my future.

I mean, I don't even have half a plan. I don't know what job

I'd do, or what hobbies I'd like. But I have to start somewhere, and for me, that's with these scribbles. Frankie's Get a Life List.

Some of them are pie-in-the-sky. Like going to Paris and seeing the pyramids in Egypt.

But some of them could be something. Like going out to dance in the city, and taking cooking classes, and learning to drive. Hell, going out dancing is something I could do tonight, if I go to Kingston's show. The flyer he gave me is smoothed out and tucked away in my underwear drawer.

I'm up and strolling through the house before I can overthink this.

I find Jamie in a rare moment of vulnerability. He's swimming laps in the pool, cutting through the water with vicious speed. He doesn't even notice me come in, my bare feet padding over the warm tiles. I lower myself down, rolling my yoga pants to the knee and dangling my legs in the water.

I can see the exact moment he notices me. He turns at the far end, plunging back towards me, then falters in his stroke. When he starts up again, he's smoother, less vicious.

Always so damn controlled.

"Got bored of stretching?" He tugs off his goggles and tosses them onto the grate. With his feet planted on the floor, the pool water laps at his heaving chest.

I drag my eyes back up to his face and find Jamie's eyes twinkling.

He's happier now we're back. Now I'm safe behind the walls. He's always sucked at staying mad.

But when I tell him, "I was thinking we could go out," his brows lower again.

"Go out where?" He asks the question carefully. Like I'm

some mental patient he has to humor.

"Dancing. To a bar." I nudge his bare hip with my toe. "You know—together."

Here's my olive branch: I won't be a brat and bust out if he'll come with me. Fair's fair.

"When?" he asks, and he's still too casual. My heart sinks, but I force myself to keep talking.

"A few days from now. In the west side of the city."

It's tonight in the south, but he's going to say no. Sure enough, Jamie's mouth presses in a tight line, and he steps an inch closer, the water lapping at my legs.

"Let's talk about it once your dad's back."

"You know what he'll say."

"Let's ask him at least."

"Why?" I swing my legs out of the pool, splashing water everywhere. I've soaked my yoga pants, but I don't care. "I'm not a child. Why do I need my dad's permission?"

"It's about your safety—"

"Bullshit." I surge to my feet and stumble, wincing at the pain in my leg. Jamie reaches for me, worry creasing his forehead, and I stagger back out of arm's length. "It's not about safety. It's about control. And you're helping him do this to me."

"I'll talk to him," Jamie begs, hand still outstretched. "We'll talk to him together. About giving you more freedom; about whatever you want."

"What I want is to go dancing. Without asking first."

Jamie spreads his palms, helpless. He looks so good, his hair dark from the swim and beads of water running down his chest. It pisses me off even more, somehow, and I snarl as I turn away.

"I'll take you, I promise," he calls at my back. The sound echoes around the pool. "Just as soon as your father's home."

"Don't bother," I mutter under my breath.

If he won't take me, I'll take myself.

* * *

One upside of being a prisoner in your own home is you know the place by heart. I know where every camera, every guard route, and every exit is. I know what times the guards swap over, and how often Jamie checks on me.

If he's suspicious, he doesn't show it. He spends the day trying to coax me into a better mood, cooking me pancakes for a late breakfast and sitting out in the garden while I work through my exercises. My emerald toe nails sparkle up at me, a constant reminder that Jamie can be sweet.

My plans don't change. There's another sweet man playing in a bar tonight.

I head to bed earlier than usual, yawning and stretching my arms. It makes sense that I wouldn't want a movie marathon with Jamie. It makes sense that I'd be tired after the last few days.

He still checks on me twice more than usual, poking his head into my pitch black bedroom. The light from the hall casts weird shadows on his face, and he stays long enough to hear my breathing.

Right. Okay. I slide my laptop out from under my bed as soon as he's gone. I set it to record and breathe into the mic, slow and steady like I'm asleep.

It won't fool him for long, but it might buy me some precious minutes.

I leave it playing on a loop, the screen set to black, and head out through my bathroom window. It's a tight fit, and my skinny jeans don't help, but I'm dressed to the nines tonight. If I only have a few hours of freedom, I'm sure as hell making the most of them. I scrabble at the trellis with my sandals, ivy leaves tickling my feet.

It's not smooth—Jamie will scoff when he sees the replay on the cameras—but I drop the last foot to the grass and dust myself off.

New phone: check. ID and cash: check. Flyer: triple check.

No need for keys. As if the guards would refuse to let me back in.

The outer wall is trickier, but I've had years in this garden to picture my great escape. Jamie and I used to make a game of it, challenging each other to come up with more and more ridiculous heist plans.

I bet he'll kick himself for that after tonight.

There's a wrought-iron gate set into a garden wall. It's not an outer wall, so no one thinks anything of it. But you can climb up the iron swirls and use it to scramble on to the gardener's shed.

It's a two-foot leap between the gardener's shed and the garage roof.

And from the garage roof, you can slide down nice and easy onto a thick, springy hedge.

I thud onto the dirt, the hedge scratching at my arms, on the other side of our garden wall. Our driveway curves for half a mile through the trees before it reaches the street. I set off at a wobbly jog, plucking leaves from my hair and scanning for the headlights of my cab.

* * *

The bar door is propped open, strains of music floating into the street. I pay the cab driver and slam the door shut, lingering on the sidewalk. It's a cool night, the baking sun long gone, and the smokers gathered out in the breeze are bundled up in jackets. The ends of their cigarettes flare orange one by one as they each take a drag.

"You lost, sweetheart?" says a man in his thirties. I wrinkle my nose. I only like it when Kingston calls me that.

I dig the flyer out of my back pocket and smooth it flat between my palms. AJ's Place; the blues bar. This is it.

"Nope."

I skirt around the smokers and march up the three steps. The buzz of conversation, the clink of glasses and pool balls, the music—it hits me like a wall. I blink hard, sucking in a deep breath and ducking my head to push through the crowds. There's a deep, gravelly voice singing into a microphone somewhere, and the jumble of lamps and spotlights cast half the bar in shadow.

Hands brush against my hips as I make my way to the bar, and I smack a couple away. Still, a grin stretches over my cheeks by the time I lean my elbows on the wood.

"Whisky," I call, when the bartender looks at me. I've never had one before, but this is a whisky kind of night. Dark and hot and dangerous, with strangers pressing close all around.

The tumbler lands in front of me, amber liquid sloshing up the sides, and I slap the cash into the barman's palm.

One sip, and I'm spraying the man next to me. Maybe I'm not a whisky girl after all.

"You get used to it."

I know that voice. I shivered in my bed last night playing it over in my mind. I spin on my heel, and sure enough, there he is: Gabriel Ortiz, leaning up against the bar. He's stood facing the crowd, resting his elbows on the wood, and he's even finer than I remember.

A nearby lamp casts a glow over his face, lighting up his golden brown skin. He's clean-shaven, his salt and pepper stubble gone, and his black shirt is fitted and pressed.

I stuff my tongue back in my mouth and look doubtfully at my glass.

"What's the point of forcing yourself to love a drink?"

Gabriel's eyes slide away from the raised stage across the room and rest on me for a second before flitting back. He shrugs.

"Some of the best things in life take more work."

I guess I wouldn't know about that. Not unless you count stowing away on riverboats, or scaling your garden walls, which I decide right on the spot that I do.

"True," I agree sagely, and take another sip. Ugh. It's even worse the second time. "Are you here to watch Kingston?"

Gabriel nods, still looking away. I fight the urge to smooth down my top. It's a black, beaded camisole, one as sultry and spooky as the city's graveyards.

"Me too," I offer. Nothing. No questions about Jamie; no rescinding my ban from his boat. The man is a brooding brick wall, and I'm sick of it after ten seconds. "Fun talk."

I clasp my drink and push through the crowd, towards the stage and away from the pointed silence. I scan the crowd for Kingston, but I don't see his warm brown eyes or cheeky smile. What I find instead is a makeshift dance floor, crammed full of spinning couples.

It's tight: elbow to elbow, with no room to go buck wild. Just smooth, precise movements among dancers who are lost in their own little world. I wedge myself in on the edge of the ring, watching them dance and soaking up the music.

The third sip of whisky goes down easier, burning all the way to my chest.

Yeah. This is what I came here for. A burning drink, the sway of hips, and the shiver of an electric guitar.

My phone buzzes in my pocket. I slide it out and check the screen.

Jamie: Are you fucking kidding me, Francesca?

I send him a smiley face in reply, then tuck it back in my pocket. I'm not an idiot. I know this phone must have a tracker. But maybe when Jamie finally catches up, he'll fancy a dance after all.

The song shudders to an end, and new musicians file onto the stage, milling around and swapping over. I glimpse Kingston, dressed all sharp in a tailored purple shirt and tight gray pants. There's no piano on the stage—the whole platform's about the size of a king-sized bed—but he slides a strap around his neck and swings a guitar into place.

"Kingston!" I yell, jumping and waving, but the crowd swallows the noise. He's focused, too, his face more serious than I've ever seen as he twiddles the little knobs and tunes his guitar. Watching his elegant fingers play over the strings, I take another sip of whisky.

He's something else. One of those people with a whole boatload of talent, and humble with it, too. I shift my weight as I watch him, pressing the cool of my glass against my hot neck.

"He plays the fiddle, too. And the drums."

I throw a glance at Gabriel, looming beside me in the crowd. Then I turn back to watch Kingston setting up, ignoring him the same way he ignores me.

Barely a minute passes before the music starts up again. It begins with the shiver of cymbals, then the steady thump of drums. Kingston's guitar joins, low and sensual, and the other musicians leap in one by one. The dancers find the beat, scooping up each other's hands and slotting their legs together, and then the makeshift dance floor is full of spinning couples once more.

I sway to the beat, grinning up at Kingston and tossing my hair out of my eyes. He scans the audience as he plays, a tiny crease in his forehead the only sign of his concentration. When his eyes land on me, his whole face lights up, and I beam at him like a megawatt spotlight. I jump, holler and wave like the world's most embarrassing soccer mom, but he takes it all in his stride, nodding and holding my gaze like he's playing just for me.

The song morphs, changing into another number. Kingston looks away, glancing around at the rest of the band, and it breaks the spell. I rock back on my heels, cheeks flushed, and the room fades back into existence.

"Welcome back," Gabriel says dryly. I ignore him and toss back the last gulp of my drink. It scorches a trail all the way down my chest, but I'm glad for the buzz it gives me. I feel lighter as I lean around a man's back and plonk my empty glass on a table.

"He's incredible."

Gabriel hums. "That he is. Kingston's too good for my boat, really, but too loyal to move on."

"You should kick him out. You know: in a nice way, once he's got something better lined up."

Gabriel leans closer, his arm pressing against mine, and tips his chin to murmur in my ear.

"You didn't like it when I kicked you out."

I nudge him in the ribs with the pointy part of my elbow.

"Because you didn't do it nicely."

A dancing couple spins past so close I stumble backwards to keep from being stepped on. Gabriel huffs, taking my arm, and pulls me right into the center of the swaying bodies.

"We're in the way."

He presses a palm against my lower back and guides my legs to slot between his.

"No, we're not."

I bite my lip so hard it hurts, focusing on the sliver of collarbone visible behind his open collar. Dancing with Kingston, I was confident. Cool. With Gabriel, I have to take long, slow breaths to force myself to calm down.

Get it together, Frankie. He's not your boss anymore.

He's so solid, his shoulders broad and his thighs thick with muscle, that I feel like a koala clinging to a tree. But he's graceful too, spinning us in languid circles to the beat.

"You don't limp when you dance."

I frown at the cleft of his chin.

"I guess I'm distracted."

His hand slides tighter against my back, cinching me closer, and there's no way he can't feel my heart thundering in my chest. I risk a glance and find him watching me, eyes dark and heated, and without thinking I press closer. I rock up onto my toes, palm sliding along his shoulder to his neck, and tilt my face towards him.

For a long, impossible moment—the space between beats—I think he's going to kiss me. His eyes are hooded, his chest heaving under mine, and we're sealed against each other.

Then Gabriel blinks and rears back, his nostrils flaring, and it's like a bucket of cold water tossed down my neck. We finish the dance, turning and swaying like everyone else, but it's clinical. Detached. I'm relieved when the song draws to an end and I can pull away, a lump stuck in my throat.

"Thanks," I croak, forcing a polite smile, then turn on my heel and plunge back into the crowd.

A drink. I need another drink. And a nice long break from Gabriel Ortiz.

* * *

I take an embarrassingly long time to notice, but the bar has two levels. The bottom floor is packed: a surging mass of hot, sweaty bodies and tipped drinks. But in the corner of the room, through a door next to the coat check, there's a quiet stairwell leading to an even quieter second floor.

I squeeze the wooden handrail tight, forcing out a breath as I climb the stairs. I may not limp when I dance, but I sure pay the price for that later. But the chaos downstairs is getting to me—the wall of noise, the press of sweaty shirts—and I'd rather grit my teeth through this climb than cower downstairs in the corner.

It's worth it. The upstairs has an empty, shadowed hallway, a ladies' bathroom, and curtained gaps in the wall leading to theater-style boxes overlooking the stage. I duck under a dusty red velvet curtain and collapse into a squashy chair, gusting out a sigh of relief.

My leg throbs something awful, singing up at me like the man crooning onstage. Kingston's set is long finished, and I stayed downstairs long enough to catch up with him fresh from his show.

"I'm so happy you're here!" he cried out, squeezing my shoulders, and you could tell from the sparkle in his eyes that the sweetheart meant it. He was hot from playing under those spotlights, his forehead beaded with sweat and his damp shirt sticking to his back. He didn't smell bad, though. When he gathered me in for a tight hug, he smelled damn near lickable.

Gabriel watched us, silent and unreadable as ever, before pushing a fresh beer into Kingston's hand.

"Boss Man." Kingston tipped his chin, using my nickname for the grumpy older man. Gabriel glowered at my cackle.

Up in the relative quiet of the second floor, I catch my breath. I tip my head back against the faded upholstery and close my eyes, feeling the thrum of my pulse.

Three drinks. Too many dances to count—some with Gabriel, some with Kingston. And no sign of Jamie, even though I figured he'd be here hours ago.

An idiotic part of me is kind of hurt. Worried that he's given up on me. But he's a professional bodyguard, not a boyfriend. He slips through the curtain and lowers into the next chair over.

"You look dead on your feet."

I slide him a look, smoothing down my crazy hair. When I checked my makeup in the bathroom mirror, I looked like a raccoon.

"How long have you been here?"

"Since ten minutes after your text."

I nod and settle back against the seat. It was nice of him, in a repressed sort of way, to let me stay and drink and dance. Would have been better if he'd removed the stick up his ass and joined in, but baby steps. Baby steps.

"You case the joint?"

He snorts. "What does that even mean?"

I shrug. "You know, like in movies. Checking all the exits or whatever."

"I'm not a complete idiot, Frankie."

I tip my head and smirk at him.

"Whoever said you were?"

We settle into companionable silence. The same quiet we share when we're reading on the back porch, or cooking breakfast in the morning. Jamie started feeling like home to me a long time ago, and it soothes the ache in my chest just to have him near.

"Carrick is going to hate your new boyfriends," he blurts.

I wrinkle my nose. "I danced with them. I didn't ask them to prom."

"Just as well. Your older fella would never get in."

I slap his arm. "He's not old. He's distinguished."

I don't know why I'm so quick to leap to Gabriel's defense, except that I don't want anyone calling him old. If he's old, then that makes me some sort of pervert, and I don't have the bluster to carry that off.

"He's twice your age, Frankie."

"Well, you're ten years older." The silence morphs just like that: from soothing to tense. It takes far too long for Jamie to speak, and when he does, he sounds all kinds of strained.

"I'm your bodyguard, Francesca. Nothing more."

Hurt ripples through my chest. Nothing more? So all those mornings cooking waffles or home fries together; all those nights spent squashed up on the sofa watching movies—they were work for him?

"Good to know." I say it quietly, but I know he hears. I draw my legs up and rest my chin on my knees.

God damn Jamie. It was such a good night until he came into this box.

"Frankie," he says, like he's pleading with me. I grit my teeth and stare down at the stage. "Frankie," he says again, hand reaching for me, and I've had enough. I stand before he can touch me.

"Let's go. I've had enough for one night."

He doesn't look happy, but he stands and follows me out of the box. He says nothing as I take forever to shuffle-walk down the stairs.

I won't meet his eye. He hurt me badly, and he knows it. He damn well knows it.

I should be polite and find the others to say my goodbyes. To congratulate Kingston one more time on his performance. But the sea of strange bodies is loud and grasping, and I can't bring myself to go back in there again. Not tonight.

I shoot Kingston a text instead, ignoring Jamie trying to read over my shoulder. And I send Gabriel one too—a single sentence. *See you around, Boss Man.*

"All right." And it is all right when Jamie takes my elbow and leads me out through the doorway. The fresh air slaps my cheeks awake, and my feet drag over the sidewalk as he takes me to his car.

Jamie goes to open my door, gripping the handle, but he stalls, his jaw clenched tight.

"About what I said—"

"Don't worry about it." I nudge him out of the way and open the door myself. A groan slides out of my throat as I rest back against the seat, propping my leg up on the dashboard.

"Seat belt," is all Jamie says, then he closes my door with a thump.

* * *

I can't sleep. My leg is throbbing to high hell, and a thousand thoughts are running through my mind. The estate is lonely without my parents, but their return date hangs over me like a guillotine. And after my second little stunt tonight, God only knows if Jamie will let me out of his sight again.

Jamie.

His words from the bar stew and circle in my brain, chafing over the hurt so it won't heal. I know he gets paid to look after me. I know this is his job. But I guess I was so desperate to have a real friend that I made it out to be something more.

God. How humiliating.

I toss my covers off and sit up, squinting around my moonlit bedroom. I'm surprised Jamie didn't lash me to the bed-post—Lord knows I wouldn't say no—but I guess he's confident I won't wander off again tonight. He brought us back, ran through updates with the guards, then left me standing in the lobby while he wandered off for a drink.

Fine. He can be weird about this if he likes. He can be my bodyguard, and nothing more. He doesn't owe me anything, and by the same token, I owe him nothing in return.

If we were friends, if we were more, I might give him a break. Tug my sheets back up and roll over; force myself to go to sleep.

But he said it himself: we're nothing. And I don't want to sleep yet.

I slide out of bed, my toes sinking into the fluffy rug, and pull on my thin silk robe. It's cool tonight, and my nipples peak beneath the soft fabric. I could put more layers on, sure, but this is my home. Screw it. I cram my feet in my bunny slippers and stroll to my bedroom door.

The estate never fully sleeps. There are always a few guards on duty, always lights on and the hum of voices. When Dad's home, he's always one of those awake, without fail. He barely sleeps an hour each night, he's so manic, running over businesses and ventures and plans. He always chases me back to my room when I wander at night, telling me to get my beauty sleep.

It used to piss me off, but I wouldn't mind it so much right now. It's nice to know someone cares.

I ignore the voices coming from the kitchen and turn away down the shadowed hall. I don't make a plan, I just let my feet drift, taking me wherever they want to go.

The pool. I guess my feet are thinking about Jamie too.

I'm not dressed to swim, and no way am I skinny dipping with a bunch of men down the hall. But I sit on the tiles at the edge of the pool, exactly where I sat when I talked to Jamie earlier.

My feet kick in the water, swirling currents around my legs, and my mind drifts away, distracted. Dark hair soaked from swimming. Rivulets of water streaming down a toned chest. Pale hands gripping the edge of the pool, so close to my thighs I can feel their heat.

My eyes flutter closed, and warmth throbs in my core. Even with his words still grating in my chest, I want him so badly I can't think straight.

"Trouble sleeping?"

His voice doesn't make me jump. It's like I knew he'd find me here. Jamie lowers himself to sit beside me, dressed in sweatpants and a white t-shirt for once. He rolls his sweats to his knees and dunks his feet in the water next to mine.

The most ridiculous thoughts scroll through my head. Thoughts like: the same water that touches my skin is touching him too. We're sharing breaths here, we're sitting so close. Our body heat is mingling together, warming the inches of air between us.

I don't tell him that crap. I'm not gone in the head. "I'm my father's daughter," is all I say instead.

Jamie hums and swirls his feet in the water.

"I lied before."

I nod at my knees. "Yeah, I know."

"I'm not just your bodyguard."

"I never said you were."

He sighs, like I'm making this difficult somehow. I frown at the ripples on the moonlit water, but I don't call him out on it. I wait for him to say something I can latch on to—to tell me he cares. To call me a friend. Anything.

"It pissed me off," is what comes out. "Seeing you dance with them."

I scoff. "You could have danced with me too, if you stopped skulking around."

He elbows me softly.

"Your dad would throw me out on my ear if I ever so much as sniffed you."

I turn and clap my palm against the back of Jamie's head, then hold my wrist to his nose.

"There you go," I say after a few beats, dropping my hands back to my lap. "The damage is done."

He chuckles quietly, and the sound makes me bold. I drag my legs out of the water, showering water droplets everywhere, and fumble onto my knees. When I swing a leg over Jamie's lap and settle there, he grips my hips tight with both hands.

"You're making me wet."

I raise an eyebrow. "That's called karma."

He all but chokes, and I take my chance. I slide my palms along his shoulders, up the column of his throat, and tangle my fingers in his hair. He's made of stone as I run the tip of my nose across his cheekbone and nudge it against his.

"Frankie," he grits out. "Francesca."

"Don't call me that."

I seal my mouth to his.

In all of my shameless daydreams about Jamie, he always melts under my touch. I break his fragile self-control, and he ravages me there on the spot.

He doesn't ravage me, but he doesn't push me off either. His hands squeeze my hips so hard they might bruise, and his chest heaves so much it brushes against my silk-covered nipples. I draw his bottom lip in between my teeth and nibble, relishing his sharp inhale.

Finally, he jerks me back, but it's too late for him to pretend. I can feel the evidence of how much he wants me too, hard beneath my thigh.

"We can't do this."

"Not with that attitude."

"Frankie. I'm serious."

I sigh and sit back. It takes some less than graceful maneuvering, but I tip back onto the tiles.

"I don't care about what Dad thinks. Or your job. Or your age." I address my emerald green toes, my arms wrapped around my knees.

Jamie's sigh sounds like it was dredged from the bottom of his soul.

"The world doesn't work like that, Frankie. No matter how much we want it to."

Chapter 6

I'm fully prepared to pull another Mission Impossible to get a day in the city. There are four days left until Dad's home, and you can bet your last dollar that I'm going to make the most of them.

I don't even have to, though. I get up early, running through my yoga stretches and exercises so I'm limber for my prison break. Then I wander into the kitchen for breakfast and find Jamie in jeans and a t-shirt, beating eggs in a ceramic bowl.

"Are you taking the day off?" I try to sound casual as I slide onto a stool at the breakfast bar. I couldn't blame him, not after the circus I've put him through. Jamie would be well within his rights to assign another bodyguard to me for the day and get some blessed peace.

"No." He eyes me carefully, pouring the eggs into a spitting hot pan. "I thought we could go somewhere for the day. Together."

"Really?" I rock forward, gripping the counter top with both hands. "Just us? Alone?"

Jamie grimaces, sliding a spatula under his omelet.

"Sort of. Eyes nearby. Back-up within reach. But just you and me hanging out."

You know what? I'll take it. If a few shadows in suits are

what Jamie needs to soothe his paranoia, so be it. And their presence will definitely help his case if Dad ever finds out.

"Plus, this way you won't sneak off and leave yourself vulnerable for hours at a time."

Right. God forbid we do something just for the fun of it.

"So where are you taking me?" I tap a fork against my lips, smirking as Jamie's cheeks flush pink. I'm not the only one who's been dwelling on the kiss. He slides the omelet onto a plate and pushes it to me across the counter.

"Well, there are the city gardens. Or the zoo."

I wrinkle my nose. If I only ever have one date with Jamie, I don't want to share him with a bunch of penguins. Then something Tessa told me about in our cabin leaps to mind, and I slap my palm on the counter.

"I've got it." Jamie blinks at me, eyeing the knife near my hand. "There are ghost tours in the cemetery."

His stony face melts into a grin, blue eyes shining.

"Are you serious? You want to go look at graves?"

I shrug. "Maybe we can reserve a plot next to each other."

His smile dims at that, and I wish I could take the words back, but he turns his back and starts up the coffeemaker. I chew on my bottom lip, watching his shoulder blades through his cotton t-shirt, and pull my phone out of my pocket.

Gabriel and Kingston are probably busy. And even if not, they're probably sick of me by now.

Still, it can't hurt to send a quick text. Everyone loves a ghost tour, right?

* * *

"Oh, damn it."

My ice cream drips down the inside of my wrist, leaving a sticky, creamy trail. Jamie frowns as I lick it up, holding eye contact.

"You did that on purpose."

"Did not."

"Oh, please. You've had it out for me all day."

I don't know what that's supposed to mean. As far as I can tell, I've behaved like any other girl out for the day with her grumpy bodyguard.

Did I need to wear my cutest summer dress and insist on holding Jamie's hand every chance I got?

Did I need to squeeze onto the stone wall where he's sitting, so close that I'm practically on his lap?

Yes. Yes, I very much did. And I'm not done yet, either.

"I have a surprise for you," I whisper. Jamie glares at me, visibly bracing himself for more outrageous seduction. "No, not that. You're going to hate it."

Jamie sighs. "You invited your boyfriends. I know."

I tense up, my body rigid where it's pressed against his side. "Do you read my texts?"

Because if so, this day is over. And you know what? I wouldn't put it past Dad.

"No. But one of them has been waiting over there for twenty minutes."

He nods a way down the street, to the entrance to the cemetery. Sure enough, Kingston leans against the Gothic-style railings, tapping a rhythm against his thigh. There's a tree in the cemetery behind him, and its branches are weighed down with pink blossoms.

He looks like a spring month in a hunky calendar.

I turn my glare on Jamie.

"You let him wait there all that time. That's very rude."

Jamie shrugs. "You're the one who's late for her date."

I hop down off the wall, stomach churning as I scrub at my wrist with a napkin. I don't know how I feel about Jamie calling this a date with Kingston. It's our day, too, and I want to keep Jamie square in that equation.

Can we have a group date? Is that a thing? I feel like since I've been locked in an ivory tower for eight years, I should be allowed to make up for lost time.

If Kingston's thrown off to see me arrive with another man, he doesn't show it. He hugs me and kisses my cheek like we're old friends, then shakes Jamie's hand like he's happy to meet him.

Huh. A real life gentleman. I thought they were a myth.

"Uh, is Gabriel…?" I studiously ignore Jamie's eye. Kingston's mouth twists.

"He's working. Sorry, Frankie."

As the owner of the boat, I'm sure Gabriel can come and go as he pleases. Then again, he's a full-grown man—he must have better things to do than an awkward three-way date with a college girl.

"So ghosts, huh?" Kingston twinkles down at me, one cheek dimpling, and I melt right there on the sidewalk. Even Jamie seems kind of flushed, a pink tinge dusting his cheeks.

"Ghosts, vampires, zombies: you name it. The website swears you'll be scarred for life."

Jamie snorts, and Kingston throws out an arm.

"Sounds like a treat, sweetheart. Lead the way."

* * *

The cemetery has huge sprawling grounds filled with gravestones and family tombs. There are statues everywhere you look, dotting the grass with watchful figures—angels, heroes, pilgrims, soldiers. The captains of industry. You can tell how old they are by how crumbly their stone is—some of the oldest figures practically look chewed on.

Some wealthier families have private crypts, with stone steps leading down into the earth. Others have simple, weather-worn gravestones, slumped sideways in the overgrown grass.

I wonder idly if the O'Briens have a family plot around here somewhere. Or if Jamie's parents are laid to rest in these grounds.

Shit. I didn't even think about that when I suggested this little day trip. I sidle closer to Jamie as our tour group files down the path, winding my arm through his. He smiles down at me, surprised but pleased, his face bright and untroubled. My chest loosens an inch.

All right. No family trauma here. Just a girl, her bodyguard, an indeterminate amount of plain-clothes security, and her new musician friend, out on a midday ghost hunt.

It's exactly as tacky as I'd hoped. The tour guide feeds us his script of gory tales, dressed up like a dusty vampire. We're led through dark tunnels and into abandoned crypts; jumped out on; splashed with corn syrup 'blood'.

Jamie strolls through it all, impervious and unshockable, but Kingston jerks a few times and bursts out laughing. I grin at them both, more absorbed in their reactions than the tour itself after a while.

Two hours later, we spill out of a darkened crypt onto the scraggly grass above. I bet this tour is kind of eerie in the gloomy winter months, but it's near impossible to be frightened when the trees are covered in pink blossoms and swaying in the breeze. The afternoon sun washes the grounds gold, and picks out the copper strands in Jamie's hair.

"Well?" he asks me, leading us to a quiet spot by a tree.

He tucks his hands in his pockets, his shoulders relaxed and his mouth curled in an easy smile. I don't think I've ever seen Jamie this at peace. Not in a decade. The sight steals my breath for a moment, so Kingston answers in my place.

"Spookiest two hours of my life." He nudges me. "Probably because I'm not fool enough to go wandering through graveyards after dark. That's some white people shit."

Jamie hums, and I nod in agreement.

"You have a point there."

"Movies are not on our side."

It's nice to hear them chatting. Getting along. I suck in a deep breath and scan the cemetery, feeling the soft breeze on my cheeks.

"Here it is," I blurt out, interrupting whatever they're saying. They both turn to me expectantly. "I'm not done yet. I don't want to go home."

Jamie nods, resigned, his shoulders tensing up, but Kingston clicks his tongue.

"You on the clock, man?"

Jamie nods again, mouth pressed in a line. Kingston turns to me and holds up his palms.

"Maybe we call it a day then, huh, sweetheart?"

My heart sinks. I don't have that many days.

"But—"

"How about a movie night at your place? We can watch white people go snooping through haunted houses and getting murdered. I'll mix us some drinks."

I breathe out hard. It's not what I had in mind—I wanted to stay out, see some more of the city. But now that I look at Jamie again, I can see the strain etched on his face—his tight, worried eyes and the downturn of his mouth. His eyes flick around us constantly, and his hand keeps twitching towards his hidden holster.

"Okay." Jamie's eyebrows shoot up. Is it that shocking for me to agree? I can be reasonable, damn it. I just don't appreciate being caged. "So long as you go to town on these drinks. I'm talking umbrellas and shit. The works."

Kingston beams. "You got it."

* * *

There's something so freaking intimate to having someone over at your house. I don't remember the last time someone came to visit me at home. Maybe a school tutor? A physio for my leg? It's a depressing thought.

It's even weirder to see the estate through a stranger's eyes. There's barely anything of me here outside my room. The decoration is all in Mama's style—or at least, it's to her interior decorator's taste. Everything looks like the inside of a magazine: perfect and bland and cold. All neutral colors, stylish rugs, and artfully placed standing lamps.

It never bothered me before tonight, but as we lead Kingston inside, I feel kind of itchy. His gaze tracks over the marble lobby, the oil paintings on the walls, and he doesn't stop looking with that careful, blank expression as we lead him into the kitchen.

Jamie doesn't seem bothered at all. He's cool and unruffled, as always. But I guess this is his employer's house, not his family home. Not the building he's spent most of the last eight years inside.

Was it always this lifeless? Where the hell have I been?

Whatever he might think, Kingston's too polite to say it. He follows Jamie straight into the kitchen, clapping the other man on the back as he gathers supplies for cocktails. Jamie sets a pan of popcorn on the hob and fills a bowl with nachos.

I just stand there and stare, like a prize idiot. I will myself to move, to say something, but I'm suddenly so shy I'm struck dumb.

"You've done it," Jamie tells Kingston. "You've done the impossible. Francesca's piped down."

That snaps me out of it..

"Don't call me that."

He chuckles.

I slide onto a breakfast bar stool and watch them move around each other in the kitchen. They flow together so easily, always out of each other's way, that it reminds me of that makeshift dance floor.

I keep that observation to myself. They've had enough frights for one day.

Kingston sets a glass on the counter in front of me and wanders off to put on some music. I inspect my drink: a vivid fade from blood red at the base to pale orange.

"Tequila sunrise," Jamie tells me, sliding the bowl of chips over too.

"Duh," I say, though I had no clue.

It's sweet but tart, with sugar crusted on the rim. I lick my lips and suck down another gulp.

"Easy, tiger." Jamie winks at me. "You've got all night, remember?"

He's talking about movies. He probably means nothing by it. But his words send a bolt of heat straight to my core, and I squirm on the seat of my stool.

"You're going to stay with us, right?"

Jamie smirks at me, his eyes dark.

"Well now, I can't leave you with a strange man, can I?"

Can he? Could he? I'm so out of my depth in this conversation, I open and close my mouth like a goldfish. Kingston rescues me from the other side of the room, switching on a slow, moody track. It fills the kitchen, covering my silence, and pulsing over my goose-pimpled skin.

Shit. Shit, shit, shit. I swallow hard, shifting on my stool. Jamie watches me, a sinful smile quirking his mouth.

"What movie do you want to watch?" Kingston asks, coming to stand by my shoulder. I clear my throat and force myself to think straight.

Nope. Not happening. Not with Kingston's delicious scent filling my nose, and with Jamie watching me like something to eat.

"You pick," I tell him weakly, flipping Jamie off when he chuckles.

It's going to be a long night.

* * *

Squashed onto the sofa between Jamie and Kingston, I barely even notice the movie. The screen flickers in front of my eyes, but my stare is glassy and unseeing. The sounds buzz in the background, but my brain can't make out the words.

I'm so freaking aware of both of them, there's no room for anything else. The steady rise and fall of Jamie's chest. The hard line of Kingston's arm against mine. The calluses on his knuckles and fingertips from playing instruments, compared to the scars notching Jamie's hands.

I glance down at my own fingers, twined in my lap. I had to tangle them there to stop myself from reaching for both of them. They're pale, unmarked and unchallenged, except for one scratch I got working on the boat.

One scratch. One tiny, scabbed red line. That's the only sign on me that I've been living.

That, and the warped scar tissue on my leg, I guess. But that was inflicted, not earned. It doesn't count.

Jamie nudges me gently.

"You're missing all the fake blood."

I blink up at the screen. "Sorry."

I rub my thumb over the knuckles of my other hand, pretending to watch the film.

Does it feel different when the person touching you has calluses? Scars? Are the only marks on Jamie on his hands, or are there more on the rest of his body?

I didn't get a good look in the pool—I was too distracted by the water streaming down his chest. He looked like the newer statues in the cemetery: carved from stone in perfect, godlike proportions.

Jeez, it's a good thing he can't read my mind. His ego would never recover.

Kingston shifts on the sofa, his thigh pressing up against mine. His warmth bleeds through his jeans, the sculpted shape of him clear even through the fabric, and my mouth goes dry. I clench my fingers tighter together, fusing my eyes to the random shapes on the screen.

A hand rests on my grasped fingers, the pressure soft and

warm.

"Relax," Kingston murmurs. "It's just a movie."

I nod, not looking at him. My fingers don't unwind.

"Would you like me to go?"

Jamie shifts on my other side, leaning forward. Getting ready to stand.

"No!" I sound more strangled than the woman dying on screen, but they both sit back. Two pairs of eyes watch me. I clear my throat and try again.

"I'm just nervous."

"Why?" Jamie slides an arm around the back of the sofa. It's protective.

I shrug and reach for my drink on the coffee table with a shaking hand. It slides down my throat, cool and soothing, and the burn of alcohol is exactly what I need.

"I haven't done this much." I set the glass down with a thud and glance at Jamie. He frowns at me.

"Watched a movie?"

"No." I turn and place a hand on Kingston's cheek. The scruff on his jaw tickles my palm, and I feel his face shift as he smiles. "This."

Kingston hums, low and sensual, as I pull his face to mine. I kiss him, softly at first, then slow and deep, the ache in my core building to an insistent throb. On my other side, I hear Jamie starting to leave and I fling out a hand. I grab a fistful of his shirt, holding him here. Holding him with me.

"You said you'd stay," I gasp out when we break apart. Kingston leans over me, eyes boring into mine, but I turn and shake my hand in Jamie's shirt.

He watches me, jaw tensed so hard his teeth might crack. When I flatten my palm on his chest, he's rigid with tension.

Jamie's eyes flick past me to Kingston. Whatever he sees there, over my shoulder, it makes up his mind. He looks back at me, conflict churning in his eyes, his mouth twisted in a grimace.

Then he snaps.

Jamie scoops an arm behind my waist and hauls me up to straddle his lap. I go gladly, sucking in a shocked breath, and brace my hands on his shoulders. An arm bands around my back and tugs me close, sealing me against him. Our bodies surge against each other with every hard breath, and I groan and press even closer.

The hard length of his cock lines up with my core. I whimper and grind my hips down.

"Jesus Christ."

Jamie fists a hand in my hair and jerks me down for a kiss. It's bruising and desperate—the product of years' worth of frustration. I give as good as I get, plunging my tongue into his mouth then pulling back to nip at his bottom lip.

Vaguely, I remember we're not alone, and I pat along the back of the sofa with one hand. For a second, I'm worried Kingston has gone. That this is too much for him. But then my fingers connect with a hard chest and a warm shirt, and I tug him closer to sit right at Jamie's side.

"Well, that's something," he murmurs as we break apart, resting our foreheads together. Jamie stares up at me like I'm his whole world, his hands gripping tight at my thighs.

I tip my head and grin at Kingston.

"I knew he was into me."

Kingston snorts. "Sweetheart, the entire city knew."

Jamie looks disgruntled, but when I grind down again he lets it go real fast. His hands slide up my hips and squeeze at my waist.

"Frankie," he breathes.

"Do you like this?" I glance at Kingston. "Do you both like this?"

Kingston cracks a lazy smile. Jamie swallows hard, then nods. He jumps when Kingston cards his fingers through his hair, but after a second he leans into the other man's touch.

"Your boy here is wound awful tight, sweetheart."

I hum and kiss Jamie's neck. "I know."

"We could help him unwind together, you and I."

Beneath my ass, Jamie's cock gets impossibly harder. Still, I sit back and catch his eye. My thumb strokes over his cheekbone, so adorably pink.

"What do you think?"

Jamie sucks in a shuddering breath and holds it. His eyes flick between Kingston and I, then he collapses back against the sofa.

"Yes." He swallows. "Yes. But not in here. There are cameras here."

Kingston's head jerks up as he frowns around the ceiling, but I level Jamie a look.

"And whose fault is that?"

He rolls his eyes, but doesn't let go of me as he stands. He hitches me up, one hand holding my ass and the other wrapped around my back. I twine my legs around his waist, relishing the feel of his hard body, and nibble his earlobe as he leads Kingston down the hall.

Not to my room. To Jamie's private quarters. I raise my eyebrows, pulling back to glare at him.

"Does this mean there are cameras in my bedroom?"

He huffs, like he's offended by the question.

"No. It means no guards patrol by here."

I nod, mollified, and try my best to wipe that grumpy expression off his face. Starting with sucking a bruising kiss into the pulse point on his throat.

Jamie groans, his arms banding around me tighter, and I smirk against his skin.

He'll never stay grumpy again.

* * *

"Here."

Jamie lowers me on to my feet just as Kingston steps up behind me. Jamie's room is less bland than the rest of the house—there's a bookcase crammed with worn paperbacks, their spines creased and fading, and a surprising array of potted plants. It would be sweet, except for the collection of daggers hung on one wall.

"Do you ever use those?" I jerk my chin at the blades.

Jamie scoffs. "Of course not." Okay, good. "I keep my proper knives in my safe."

Kingston's chest rumbles behind me, and I remember that he's not exactly in the loop about Jamie's job. Yes, he works as my bodyguard and as estate security, but he does… other stuff for my father.

I'm not even sure what stuff, to be honest. Something tells me ignorance is bliss.

Besides, off-duty Jamie is a pussycat. When I draw my flattened palms down his chest and over the ridges of his abs, he practically purrs and leans into my touch. Kingston draws my hair away from one shoulder and presses a kiss into my neck.

God. It's… overwhelming. Being bracketed by two hard chests, two men, and all their focus on me. And not just two strangers, but sweet, gorgeous Kingston, and the man I've been pining after for years.

Jamie.

His eyes lock onto mine, searing straight into my soul, and any leftover fears I have about whether he wants to share evaporate into a fine mist. His gaze burns me, his grip tight on my waist, and I watch as he stares at Kingston nibbling my neck, his pupils blowing wide.

"You taste so sweet." Kingston licks a stripe up my skin, and I shiver, pressing back against him. "Sweet as peaches."

"It's to trick you. Hide her poison." Jamie smirks at me, teasing, and I poke my tongue out.

"We can't all be bitter."

He tugs me away from Kingston until I'm plastered against his chest.

"No, we can't."

My experience with men so far consists of a few hurried encounters in the gardens. On late nights when Dad was away from town, and I could risk dragging one of the gardener's boys behind the ornamental hedges.

Those times were fun, don't get me wrong. There's a special thrill when you're scared of getting caught.

But there's no one here to catch us tonight. The highest authority in this house is Jamie. And he's sure as hell not stopping, not as he leads us slowly towards his big bed.

It's kind of vanilla—a bed. After all those times rolling in the dirt. But I guess I should try it at least one time.

"I've never done this in a bedroom before," I announce, crawling up onto the mattress. Jamie growls, taking hold of my ankles and pulling my legs out from under me. He leans down, his chest against my back, and murmurs in my ear.

"Do I want to know what you've been up to, Francesca?"

I snicker. "I don't know. Do you?"

He growls again and flips me over, yanking my legs until my ass rests on the very edge.

"I'd like to hear it," Kingston says, winking at me from over Jamie's shoulder. I open my mouth to spill all the juicy details, but Jamie slides his hands up my dress and hooks his fingers around the waistband of my leggings.

"Wait." I put my hand on top of his and he stills, watching me carefully. "Don't pull them past my knees."

He knows exactly what I'm hiding—the scars on my legs—and his mouth twists in disapproval, but he nods. He won't push me, even though I can practically hear the words on the tip of his tongue.

I know I need to get over it at some point. But not tonight. Baby steps.

True to his word, Jamie rolls my leggings down to my knees and not an inch further. I lift my hips to help him, and once they're down, he flips up the skirt of my dress.

The room is warm and still. There's no breeze, but I still feel a phantom chill on my bared underwear.

"Beautiful girl," Kingston murmurs, stroking a hand up my thigh, then tracing delicate patterns just below my hip.

"Wilful girl," Jamie corrects him, pressing a hand into my stomach. "Hold her down."

I sink back into the pillows, fisting my hands in the bed covers, and force myself to breathe through the sensation of two sets of hands touching me. Jamie's lips skating up my leg. Kingston's fingers teasing my underwear down. The pair of them move in perfect harmony, like this is a choreographed dance and not the work of an impulse.

"Frankie," Jamie whispers against my skin, sucking a bruise into my hip.

His mouth drifts across my bare form, before licking a stripe along my core. I cry out, tangling one hand in his hair and scrabbling for Kingston with the other. Our gorgeous musician slides his talented fingers inside me, working my body higher and higher.

"She's so damn decadent," he murmurs. "Is she always like this?"

Jamie ignores him, working me over with his tongue. If Kingston thinks we're always together, I won't correct him.

As far as I'm concerned, I've been Jamie's for a long time. And he's been mine.

But that doesn't mean there's not room for more, especially when Kingston runs his spare hand up Jamie's back. He traces a line from the base of his spine, up between the bodyguard's shoulder blades. Jamie shudders under his touch, licking me harder and pressing his hard cock against my knee.

Yeah. There's plenty of us to go around. And now that I've got him, I'm eager to share. Jamie may have more freedom to come and go, but he's been locked away here for years, same as me.

He makes up for lost time now, lathing me with his tongue, coaxing the flames in my core hotter and hotter. I lay back and moan and breathe as best I can, and when Kingston crooks his fingers inside me, I break.

I clamp down on Kingston's fingers, shock waves rushing through me as I buck under Jamie's hold. He keeps licking me, wringing every second of pleasure out of me, until I slump back against the mattress.

"Have mercy." I bat them both away, then toss my forearm over my eyes. I'm boneless, turned to a puddle of jelly, and my ears are ringing.

It was never like that in the gardens.

I guess that's score one to beds.

"This is classic Frankie," Jamie says to Kingston as they both stretch out on either side of me. "She pushes and pushes, but half the time she can't take what she's asking for."

I crack one eyelid, glaring at his smirking face. His chin's still slick.

"Those are big words from the world's most repressed man."

Jamie pinches my waist, but Kingston reaches over and rubs his thumb over Jamie's shining lip. That shuts us up in record time, both stilling and watching to see what he'll do next.

"Don't be bitter, sweetheart," Kingston murmurs, and hearing him call Jamie that does something to me. I press my thighs together, the ache starting back up in my core. "You'll get your relief, same as Frankie here."

Jamie darts his tongue out to Kingston's thumb. His voice is rough when he speaks.

"Promises, promises."

Kingston looks down at me, a wicked smile stretching his cheeks.

"Where would you like to begin?"

We both gaze at Jamie from head to toe, taking in his creased clothes, flushed cheeks and bright eyes.

I rest my head back against Kingston's shoulder and take a deep breath.

"Everywhere," I tell them both, raw honesty making my voice hoarse. "I want all of him."

Chapter 7

Three days until Mom and Dad come home, and I'm all set to make an impassioned speech to Jamie. Something stirring and inspirational, about how I can't go back to the way things were.

About how I won't hide away on the estate anymore. How I won't give Kingston up.

I won't give Jamie up either.

We spent the night entwined in his bed, tangled up in a pile of limbs. Even when it got overheated and stuffy, Jamie stomped across the room and threw open a window rather than make us leave.

It was perfect. I barely slept an hour, but it was perfect.

Kingston ducked out before the sun rose, kissing us both on the lips and promising to see us soon. He had an early shift on the boat and had to check on his little brothers before going to work.

When he said that, I realized I barely know a thing about Kingston outside of his work. Well, that and the way he tastes. What he sounds like when he comes. In any case, I resolved on the spot to get to know him better. I want to hear it all.

His favorite movie. His ultimate comfort food. How he started working on a boat anyhow.

But it all has to wait for another day, another stolen interlude. Kingston bids us both goodbye and slips out of Jamie's bedroom door, out into the shadowed hall.

There are no shouts from security guards. No shriek of alarms. That's a good sign, right?

Never mind that the whole house knows what we were up to last night. If Dad doesn't already know, he will soon.

The same thought must have occurred to Jamie, because he rolls out of bed with a heavy sigh. He says nothing—doesn't even look at me—just makes a beeline straight to the shower.

Fine. He can be a repressed idiot again if he must. I'm used to hot and cold from him. But I can't help gritting my teeth as I slide out of bed and throw last night's clothes back on.

Okay. I didn't expect rose petals and sonnets. And he already makes me breakfast most mornings. But would it kill him to express a single emotion? To not bottle up every damn thing?

I thump the flat of my hand against his bathroom door on my way out.

"Jamie!"

The spray of the shower drums against the floor. Nothing.

Sighing, I slip through his bedroom doorway and through the halls. I take my sweet time strolling to my room—I won't hide away or be ashamed. I've done nothing wrong. We're all consenting adults, and besides—last night was perfect.

Too bad about this morning. Damn it, Jamie.

I shower, change, and work through my exercises in the privacy of my bedroom, wincing at the ache in my leg. I've been pushing it, forcing it to dance and walk for hours, not to mention rolling around with both guys last night. We didn't... do *that,* but we took turns making each other come like it was the orgasm Olympics.

The sensible thing to do would be to ease off. Slow down. Take a day to rest up and reflect.

But I don't have a spare day. I'm on the clock, counting down until the shit hits the fan. No way am I spending those precious free hours splayed out on the sofa.

"We need to talk."

Jamie comes in without knocking, his hair damp from the shower. It's combed, neat and precise, and his jaw is clean-shaven; his shirt bright white and pressed. He fiddles with the cuff of his sleeve, doing up those tiny buttons.

I flop back on my yoga mat, staring up at the ceiling.

"Well, this sounds fun."

"What happened last night… it can't happen again, Francesca."

I swallow hard around the sudden lump in my throat. Tears burn at the back of my eyes and I blink them away. He doesn't get to see me cry.

"Of course it can't." I'm proud of how steady my voice sounds. "You'd have to put me above my dad, and that will never fucking happen."

I can hear his sigh, though I don't look away from the ceiling. There's a strand of cobweb floating next to the light.

"It's not about choosing sides."

"I never stood a damn chance."

"Will you stop?"

I lurch up onto my elbows. "Yes. I will. I'll stop the second you leave my fucking room."

I'm hissing, all my hurt and rage coming through, but I can't help it. Jamie's face crumples, regret and sadness in his eyes, and my teeth are practically vibrating with how mad I am.

How dare he act like the wounded one? He's the damn

coward.

"Where do you want to go today?" he asks at last, like it's a peace offering. My answer comes easily.

"Away from you."

He nods, eyes dropping to the floor. "You'll have to take one of the other guards—"

"No."

"Francesca—"

"I said no." I'm done being bossed around. "If you or any of the others follow me, I'll call the cops. I have a goddamn right to privacy."

"I'll have to call your father."

I throw up my hands. "So call him. Tell him I'm moving out while you're at it."

I scramble to my feet, teeth gritted, and the fact that I'm so slow, so clumsy in my movements makes me so mad I could spit.

I snatch up my belongings like they each wronged me in a past life, rough and irreverent. Then I march to the bedroom door, blocked by my ashen-faced ex-bodyguard.

"Move." I'm not messing around. If he wants to keep me here, he'll need to become the jailer he's always denied being.

Jamie hovers, indecision warring on his face, and for a second I think he'll actually do it. Bundle me inside, lock my bedroom door, and cage me here like an animal.

He steps aside, nostrils flaring.

"If this is because I won't sleep with you again—"

I burst out in peals of cruel laughter. I whirl on him once I'm safely in the hall, walking backwards towards the lobby.

"Don't flatter yourself. Right at this moment, I wouldn't touch you with a ten-foot pole."

"You're being ridiculous. You know how dangerous this is. Do you really want a damn tantrum to get you killed?"

I shrug, throwing my arms up. "Better than wasting my life away in this house."

I reach the doorway to the lobby and turn to leave. Then I pause, look back over my shoulder, and add: "Oh, and Jamie? I mean this. Go to hell."

* * *

On the one hand, my dramatic exit is years overdue. Hurt burns in my chest, and I breathe hard with every step as I charge out that house.

On the other hand, my planning skills leave a lot to be desired. The O'Brien estate is in the hills on the outskirts of town. I don't have a car, and couldn't drive one even if I did, and cabs take thirty minutes to come all this way.

My mood deserves the squeal of tires on the driveway and maybe a few dents in one of Dad's precious cars. Instead, I slump against the estate's outer walls and call round the cab companies. I pinch the bridge of my nose as I talk, screwing my eyes shut and forcing myself to sound normal.

Friendly. Pleasant. Sane.

Not one more taunt away from committing first degree murder.

None of the guards follow me off the estate, so at least Jamie's not having me tailed. But one of the security cameras swivels on the wall until its lens points straight at me.

I flip it off and sweep my hair over my shoulder, blocking my face. Then I plant my feet, cross my arms, and wait.

I'm getting the hell out of here.

CHAPTER 7

Out of all the myriad places in the city, there's only one place I want to go. One place where people know my face, where people give half a damn about me. I bite out the address as I slide into the backseat of the cab, and when we get close to the river, I wind down my window.

Freshwater breeze rolls into the car, muggy and earthy and cool. I screw my eyes shut, feel the air on my cheeks, and breathe. Breathe.

My heart's still jack rabbiting in my chest when I hustle up the riverboat ramp. I stumble to a halt and buy a ticket—I may technically still be banned, but at least I paid my way this time.

I run a finger along the edge of the credit card as the man in the booth prints my receipt. It's a family credit card, and the little printed name says Carrick O'Brien. Everything in my life is paid for by my parents. I've got nowhere to go, no way to live.

Not yet, I tell myself, and straighten my spine. That's all going to change, starting today.

I take my receipt and ticket with muttered thanks and a strained smile, then wander onboard the riverboat. The sickly, churning feeling in my stomach tells me to find Kingston and his soothing words. But my feet turn in a different direction, leading me up the narrow stairs to the top deck.

It takes me two false turns in the rabbit warren corridors, but I finally find Gabriel Ortiz's office. I knock softly on the wood, but there's no answer. I figured there wouldn't be. It's early, and the boat is setting off in ten minutes. Gabriel is probably prowling around, giving orders and keeping a watchful eye.

It's wrong of me. Not to mention a long shot. But I test the door handle to his office, just to see.

It turns in my grip, stiff but yielding. I nudge the door open and limp inside.

What is it about an office that feels so damn intimate? Gabriel's not one for clutter, his desk cleared and his shelves tidied, so why does it feel like some kind of peep show being here?

Maybe because of all the insights into how his mind works. They're so obvious when you look for them. Like how all his books are arranged alphabetically by author, their spines in a precise line. How the air smells faintly of leather and spice, and how the clock on the wall is set five minutes ahead.

I lower myself into the chair behind his desk, wriggling against the cracked leather. It's squishy. Comforting. I draw my knees up and rest my forehead, closing my eyes.

The door clicks open and there's a pause. A loaded silence. Then the door thuds closed and footsteps track across the floorboards.

"You shouldn't be in here."

I grunt against my kneecaps.

"I came for a job."

"Really? This is a terrible interview."

I can't help myself. I smile against my legs, the utter ridiculousness of my morning settling over me. I dig in my shorts pocket, still not looking up, and slap my ticket onto the desk.

"I paid this time."

His laugh rumbles out of his chest. "I suppose that's an improvement."

I risk cracking one eye open, peering up at him from the chair. Gabriel leans against the bookcase, arms crossed. The sleeves of his burgundy shirt are rolled to the elbow, revealing corded forearms dusted with dark hairs. His jeans cling to his muscled thighs, and he's wearing heavy workman's boots.

"Do you do a lot of lifting in your job?" I ask doubtfully. I mean, I'm sitting behind his desk. There's a stack of yellow post-it notes.

Gabriel shrugs. "Some. And maintenance, too. That's not why I dress like this, though."

I cock my head. "Why, then?"

He smirks. "Because I'm in charge, and I want to."

He's messing with me, but his words send a shiver down my spine. I want that—that power, that self-assurance. And I want him.

I lick my lips. "Lock your door."

Gabriel raises an eyebrow but strolls across the small room to comply. It's not at all like he's obeying my command—more like he's curious. Amused. Like he'll entertain this for as long as it suits him, and not a second longer.

He turns the lock, then rests his back on the door, thumbs hooking through his belt loops.

"What's the game, Frankie?"

I ignore his question, jerking my chin at the desk.

"Sit there."

He pushes off the door, smiling darkly, and rounds the desk. He slides between my chair and the edge of the wood, settling back and splaying his legs on either side of me.

"Like this?" He quirks an eyebrow.

"Yeah. Like that." I slide my palms up his thighs, relishing the scratch of worn denim over toned legs. I reach for his belt buckle, then pause, my hand floating in the air. "This isn't about the job. This is separate."

Gabriel chuckles. "Consider the interview I never offered you paused." He smooths a lock of my hair between his thumb and forefinger, then frowns. "Where's your red-headed shadow?"

The reminder of Jamie is the last thing I want. I tug his belt open, rougher than I need to be.

"I ditched him."

"Oh?"

"He pissed me off."

"That's nothing new."

"Well, it hurt this time."

I don't spell it out, but I don't need to. Understanding dawns on Gabriel's face, and he strokes my hair again, mouth pursed in thought.

"Your date with Kingston didn't go well, then."

"It did, actually." I draw his zipper down. "You could have been there too, if you weren't so damn aloof."

"I had to work."

"You're not working now."

Gabriel opens his mouth to argue, but I draw his cock out of his boxers. It's firm under my grip, the skin hot and smooth.

He's so thick my thumb and fingers can't meet. I give a slow, teasing tug and he winds his hand tighter in my hair.

"How do you want to do this?" he asks, scratching at my scalp.

"I'm in charge." He raises his eyebrows but nods. Gabriel Ortiz is clearly not used to relinquishing control, least of all to someone half his age. I clear my throat, and add, "You can pull my hair, though. Don't be gentle. I won't break."

He smirks, guiding my lips to his cock.

"I never thought for a second you would."

He wants me to swallow him down straight away, but I drag it out. I run my lips from the base of his cock to the tip and back down again, not even kissing, just sliding over his skin. I inhale deeply, sucking the delicious, salty scent of him into my lungs. Then I dart out my tongue, lapping at the tip, and smile as he sucks in a sharp breath.

Good. I'm tired of being the one undone. I grip him firm in one fist and take him into my mouth..

Gabriel Ortiz is a large man in all ways, and it's not long before my jaw aches and my vision blurs. I keep sucking, lathing him with my tongue, my head bobbing under his tight grip in my hair. He tugs it, rough and true to his word, and my moans hum over his cock.

I slip my spare hand under the desk and rub at the seam of my shorts.

"Touch yourself," he grits out. "Do it properly."

I pull off him with a wet pop.

"I told you," I say between gasps. "I'm in charge."

But I flick my top button undone, draw down the zip and bury my hand in my shorts, sliding a finger over my core. I mutter a curse, taking hold of him again, and suck him back into my mouth.

God. He hits the back of my throat and I whimper, taking him deeper. I find a rhythm, working us both in time, and every time he grunts I squeeze my thighs tighter. I screw my eyes shut and picture how he'd feel inside me, stretching me from within. Faster and firmer, I rub at my clit, until my thighs clamp down on my hand and I fall apart.

I lose the rhythm, shaking in my chair, my mind wiped blank as I come, but Gabriel takes over. He threads his hand deeper into my hair and thrusts into my mouth, stroking a thumb over my cheekbone. I come back to myself in time to suck him hard, matching his rough thrusts and fighting for control. He grunts, his thighs tensing on either side of me, and comes down my throat.

I keep working him the whole time, easing off when he slumps back against the desk. I hum and press a kiss to the tip of his cock, then sit back in my chair.

Gabriel's cheeks are flushed; his pupils blown wide. He smirks and wipes the corner of my mouth.

"Not bad for a little rich girl."

"Or for an old man."

He chuckles and cups my face in his hands. I shift awkwardly, hyper aware of my slick, shining chin. But he leans forward, not bothered at all, and kisses me gently.

It's our first kiss, I realize, as our mouths meet. He slants his head for a better angle, thumbs tracing my jaw.

Probably should have done this before I sucked him off. But I've kissed him so many times in my mind since I saw him that first day. I guess in my brain, we've been lovers ever since, and it made perfect sense for me to jump him like this.

"Stop over-thinking," Gabriel murmurs against my lips.

I smirk and wind my arms around his neck.

"I don't know what you mean."

He coaxes me up and out of the chair until we're level, my body leaning against his. We stay there for what feels like a delicious age, kissing leisurely, rocked by the sway of the waves.

Finally, Gabriel breaks away with a sigh, and he seems genuinely regretful.

"I need to see to the boat."

I nibble at his chin.

"That's not all you need to see to."

He guides me away by the elbow, pushing to stand.

"Kingston's working the top deck bar. See if he can help you."

I don't know if that's a brush off, and I gnaw on the inside of my cheek as he strides away round the desk.

"Do you want to do this again?" I call before he reaches the door. Maybe it makes me look desperate, but I don't care. I've had enough pining to last me a lifetime.

When Gabriel smiles at me, it's the warmest he's ever looked.

"I'm not insane, Frankie. Of course I do."

I beam and he chuckles, shaking his head, then lets himself out of his office. I lower back into the chair, just to gather my thoughts, thrilled that he left me here alone. That means trust. Intimacy. Even more so than the blow job.

I kick my feet up on the desk and let out a pleased sigh.

* * *

"Hey, sweetheart." Kingston flips the dish towel onto his shoulder and leans his hands on the bar. "Jamie called. He said you might be coming."

I roll my eyes as I limp closer and slide onto a stool.

"I do not want to talk about Jamie."

Kingston hums, drawing a glass off a shelf and fixing me a drink though it's still the morning. I don't complain when he sets it down, though. I throw back that sucker like I've been walking in the desert.

Kingston chuckles and fixes me a water next. I throw that back too and set the glass down with a thud.

"You know, he told me what happened."

"Then we don't need to recap."

"He said you're gonna move out of your daddy's place."

I nod, despite my complete lack of funds, a job, or a clue.

"Yep. Gonna get out there on my own."

He whistles and sets to wiping down the bar.

"Atta girl. It's hard out there, but you've got this."

I chew on my thumbnail, wishing I believed in myself half as much as Kingston did. Hell, I've worked all of one day in my life, and got fired from that job to boot.

"I don't..." I clear my throat and try again. My voice still comes out as a whisper. "I don't know where to begin."

Kingston stops what he's doing and drums on the bar, thinking. Then he snaps his fingers and dances, jiving his shoulders to the distant strains of the radio.

"I've got it. Tessa's looking for a roommate. She doesn't sleep here most nights; she's got a place in the city."

I nod, mouth dry. Tessa's cool. I could ask Tessa.

And offer her what? A voice hisses in my brain. *Pennies for rent?*

A job. Wages. And a place to stay. I need to find all of them before Dad comes back in three days.

I sway on my stool, kind of woozy at the thought, and grip onto the bar for support. A hard chest comes up behind me, steadying me too, and I don't need to turn around to know who it is.

I know that freshwater breeze scent; those hints of spice and leather. I suck in a deep breath and lean back against Gabriel Ortiz.

"He taking good care of you?" A low voice murmurs in my ear. I tip my head back against his collarbone, and Gabriel smooths a hand up my arm.

Kingston's eyes flick over the two of us, naked interest on his face, but he doesn't seem bothered. If anything, his eyes seem to brighten.

I shrug. "He's getting me drunk before noon. That's what

you meant, right?"

"Sure," Gabriel says dryly. "Don't tell me: this is all part of your interview."

"Yep. Then I thought I'd drop a tray of glasses."

He winds a lock of my hair around his knuckle and tugs gently. The memory of what we did not long ago in his office heats up my cheeks.

"Save something for this afternoon. You're working up here with Harley."

I sit up straight and swivel round on my stool, kicking him in the shin in the process.

"Are you serious? A shift? And you'll pay me this time?"

"So long as you're not really drunk by midday."

I throw my arms around his neck and breathe into the hollow of his throat. His arms band around me a few seconds later, and he rubs a hand up my spine.

"It's not forever," he warns. "Just for today. I can't give you a job, Frankie."

"I know," I mumble into his shirt. I do know that. Besides, I don't want my first job to be somewhere I blew the boss in his office. I want to do this properly.

"Will you give me a reference?"

He squeezes me. "Sure. I've got all sorts to say."

I snort and push him off, then spin back to a grinning Kingston.

All right. This might actually work out.

* * *

The cab idles at the curb as I limp down the ramp to the docks. Every part of me aches, from my blistered feet to my stiff neck.

I've lugged full kegs of beer upstairs; scrubbed the top deck bar windows; unloaded the dishwasher hundreds of times.

I did it, though. My first ever wages are folded up in an envelope in my shorts pocket. I pluck the neckline of my black uniform shirt away from my flushed skin, fanning myself.

Gabriel told me to keep it as a memento. My first day of honest work, blow job aside. I smacked his arm when he said that, but I kept the shirt all the same.

I'm going to sleep in it and think of him. After washing it on a high heat.

The streets are still bustling at this time of night. It's late, sure, but the spring nights are warm beneath the breeze, and the bars and restaurants have their doors thrown wide open. Shafts of bright light spill onto the sidewalk, and strains of music bleed outside and clash together.

I dodge around a bachelorette party, hobbling down the sidewalk in towering heels and shrieking with laughter. On another day, I might be jealous of them—of their freedom, their camaraderie.

Not tonight. Tonight, I'm ready for a hot soak, and to studiously ignore Jamie.

"Hi there."

I muster up a smile for the cab driver, sliding into the back seat. I called in advance, never mind that the trip will eat up a big chunk of my wages.

I won't call Jamie for a ride. There's no chance in hell. I'd rather limp home the whole way. But as we pull out into the street, and the cab driver's eyes keep flicking to me in the mirror, I start to think that might have been a better option.

I clear my throat, shifting in my seat. He looks at me again. I raise my eyebrows, staring back pointedly, but he's not cowed.

If anything, his mouth ticks up in a smirk.

Nope. Hell no. Dad taught me a lot of paranoid bullshit over the years, but one thing that stuck with me is to trust my gut.

I don't like the way the driver's knuckles tighten on the steering wheel; the way he looks at my reflection then hollows his cheeks. I open my mouth to tell him to pull over, but he speaks before I have the chance.

"Carrick's out of town, huh, girlie? You don't think he'll notice you're gone?"

I tug on my car door, ready to roll into traffic, but the locks snap on. I yank harder, slapping the controls, but the door's stuck tight. Collapsing back against my seat, I breathe hard through the haze of panic.

My leg throbs hot, like some kind of alarm bell. The last time Dad's competitors took an interest in me, I wound up with these scars.

"Who are you?" I grit out.

The man chuckles. "No one you need to worry about."

Yeah, somehow I don't buy it. I clip my seat belt off and lunge at the other door, trying that handle too.

"It's locked."

"No shit." I smash my fist against the window, hard enough to jar my bones.

"Hey!" The driver finally sounds pissed. "Watch it. This car just had a full service."

I gape at the back of his headrest. Is this guy for real? Am I supposed to care about his shitty criminal cab? I turn and hammer on the glass even harder, slamming my fist against it again and again until my fingers go numb.

The guy curses and swerves to the side of the road, throwing the cab into park. He flings his door open, muttering the whole time, and marches round to my side of the cab.

The car door disappears and I topple forward, caught at the elbows by the man. He shakes me, rough, and bundles me back onto the seat, dodging my kicking feet as he straps me in.

"Get! Off!"

I lunge at him with my teeth, trying to bite his ear. But he catches my shoulders and slams me back against the seat, then pulls a cable tie from his back pocket.

"I didn't want to do this," he tells me, like I'm the unreasonable one. Then he cinches my wrists together with thick, hard plastic, so tight my fingers buzz.

"Piece of shit!" I yell after him as he ducks back out of the car and slams the door.

My wrists work against each other, but the ties only tighten. I slump back against the seat, tears brimming in my eyes, and suck in shallow, panicked breaths.

Think. Think. What would Jamie do?

I slam my heel into the driver's headrest. He jerks forward, grunting, then shakes it off and pulls back into the road. I kick at him from every angle I can manage, but he dodges me, bellowing at me to stop. I fight until my limbs are leaden with exhaustion and I'm dizzy from panic and fear.

The lights of the city flow past my window, then the darkness of the hills. I shuffle back against the corner of the cab, running over escape plans in my mind.

The cab rounds a dark corner, tree branches silhouetted against the night sky, and I blink. I know this place. By the time we pull into the estate driveway, my panic is gone, replaced with burning rage.

"Now, don't cause me any trouble."

The man pulls us to a stop by the front steps. I seethe in

silence and imagine a thousand painful deaths for him. He unlocks his door and unfolds out of the cab, murmuring to someone waiting in the shadows.

Jamie. I know him by his silhouette. From the whisper of his suit as he moves. He tugs open my car door and drops into a crouch, face cast in darkness as he unclips my belt.

"I will never forgive you for this," I tell him, voice shaking.

"I know." He sounds resigned.

"I was coming *home*."

"I know, Frankie."

"Don't call me that," I bite out. Only my friends call me Frankie.

Jamie pulls a knife from somewhere, the metal glinting in the moonlight. I hold my breath, but he slides it gently between my wrists and cuts the cable tie free. I shake out my hands, fingers prickling as the blood rushes back in.

I eye Jamie's knife, but he spirits it away somewhere in his suit, then offers a hand to help me out of the car. I gather the remaining scraps of my dignity and push past him, ignoring his hand.

The stars slide into lines overhead. I blink hard, shaking away the dizziness.

Behind me, the cab driver says something and Jamie murmurs a smooth reply, then slams him back against the car. He twists the man's arm until he screams, high-pitched and hoarse, then speaks calmly into his ear.

"If you ever lay a finger on her again, I will take you apart piece by piece. I don't give a shit who you are. Do you understand?"

The driver doesn't reply, but I guess he doesn't have to. A scream can be very convincing. I shake my head, willing this night to make sense, and let Jamie take me by the elbow and guide me up the steps.

"If you didn't want him to touch me, why send such a fucking creep?"

"I didn't," Jamie says shortly.

I don't understand. I squeeze Jamie's forearm, letting him lead me like I'm blind, and I don't let go until he deposits me on the living room sofa.

A fire crackles in the grate. It's so out of season, it can only be Jamie's doing. He loves watching the flames dance, smelling the smoke. He says it helps him think.

"I don't understand," I finally tell him. He sighs.

"Your father called. He asked to speak to you, and I had to tell him you were gone. He sent that asshole to see you home."

"Why didn't you come?"

"Would you have gotten in the car?"

"No."

"There's your answer."

I kick the sofa with my heel, mouth twisting as the panic of the last half hour bleeds away and leaves a sour taste behind.

My own father. Dad. He sent that man to 'see me home.' My wages crinkle in my pocket as I tuck up my legs.

I stare into the fire like Jamie likes to do, not moving as he tucks a blanket over my lap. He hovers for a second, tapping his thigh, then lowers onto the sofa next to me.

Not touching. Never touching. This is the story of Jamie and I: always three inches and so much unsaid between us.

"I can't stay here."

He nods. "I know, Francesca."

"Will you help me?" I swallow hard and wait an age for his reply. He leans forward, bracing his elbows on his knees, and scrubs a hand down his face.

"Yes," he says at last. "I'll help you leave."

Chapter 8

"This is so dumb, Jamie. So dumb."

He squares my shoulders, checking my stance before stepping back.

"Stop being such a baby. If you're going to strike out on your own like some modern day pilgrim, you need to know how to defend yourself. Lord knows you probably won't accept another guard."

He's right. I'm done being babysat. Maybe there is a risk to me living in the city, away from the guards and cameras of the estate. Away from Jamie. But I can't live that way anymore—cringing in fear whenever a car slows near me on the sidewalk; only emerging from the estate once a month for doctors' appointments.

Dad cleaned up his act nearly a decade ago. We used to be targets, yes—the scars on my leg attest to that. But I'm not convinced anyone's after us anymore.

We used to have smashed windows. Attempted break-ins. The alarms would go off in the middle of the night, and I'd have to fumble out of bed and slide under the frame on my belly.

No one's tried to get into the estate in years, except for one overzealous mailman.

"Try it again."

Jamie reaches for me, grabbing me in slow motion. I take a deep breath and twist in his grip, stamping down on the arch of his foot and throwing my hips back into his groin. He grunts, his hold on me falling away, and I grin as I spin back around.

"Not bad, right?"

"A little too good."

I throw up my palms. "See? I don't need this."

Jamie rolls his eyes, straightening up and wiping his hands on his shirt. He's in a tight black t-shirt, his hair glinting coppery in the daylight filtering through the garage window. He's not sweating at all or even breathing hard, his broad chest still where it stretches his shirt.

I swallow, my mouth suddenly dry.

"They won't attack you in slow motion, Francesca."

"They won't attack me at all."

I swipe my arm across my sweaty forehead. I'm so flushed, I can feel the burn of my skin, and I don't need the mirror on the wall to know I look a mess.

"You just need to know enough to get away." He's pleading, and the sad twist to his mouth makes my chest hurt. I hate when Jamie's upset. "Just long enough to call me. Or your dad, or whoever. Please, Frankie." He sighs. "Humor me with this."

I nod, falling back into the same stance he's put me in a hundred times this morning. Running over the same few self-defense drills is not how I pictured spending my precious few hours.

Getting sweaty with Jamie, on the other hand... if he weren't such a jerk last time, I'd have jumped him hours ago.

My phone chirps from my bag where it's slumped against the garage wall. I straighten back up just as Jamie lunges for me, his strong arms banding around me like a vice. I grunt and wriggle, trying to get free, everything he taught me this morning flying out of my head as soon as he touches me.

The problem is, I don't want him to get off. My traitorous body wants him closer.

I huff, screwing my eyes shut and forcing myself to ignore the barrage of sensations. His hard chest, heaving against me as he breathes. His masculine scent, enveloping me. His tight grip on me, so commanding and sure that it makes me want to melt into his hold.

Jeez. I give myself a mental kick and thrash out of Jamie's grip, breaking away and backing up until my shoulder blades hit the wall.

"Good," is all he says, a smirk tugging at his mouth. My core throbs, and I thud my head against the brick. When my phone chirps again, it's a blessed reminder, and I crouch beside my bag, cheeks flaming.

This means nothing. Just like our single night together meant nothing. All those years of wanting him, of yearning for him, and he got me out of his system in twelve hours.

"I've got to go."

I push to my feet, hooking my satchel over my shoulder. My fingers fumble as I tuck my phone away and grab my water bottle, but I can't meet Jamie's eye.

"Where?" He sounds resigned.

"To meet Kingston," I tell him, and it's true. I mean, the reason we're meeting is for a job interview with his friend, but I don't say that part.

Let Jamie be jealous. God, let him turn inside out with longing and envy.

When I look up, Jamie's face is serene. I spin around and leave without saying goodbye.

* * *

"At least he didn't follow you in the bushes."

Kingston leans back in his metal chair, gazing out across the cobbled streets. We picked an awning at random after my interview, settling in to drink coffees and play cards.

"That we know of," I mutter under my breath. I wouldn't put it past Jamie to shuffle down the street after me dressed like a mailbox.

Kingston eyes me as he deals the cards. "Why's he so paranoid anyway?"

I chew on the inside of my cheek, mulling how to get out of this conversation, but a glance at Kingston stops my excuses in my throat.

He's done so much for me. And he's told me all about his life, his brothers, his dreams. About how he wants to headline in the city's best blues bars one day, and record an album, and put his brothers through college.

I owe him this.

Sighing, I scrape the chair next to me out from under the table. Kingston watches closely as I rest my foot on the metal seat and roll up the hem of my leggings.

I hate this part.

The scars are old, but I avoid looking at them so much that they still take me by surprise, even now. The flesh is warped and uneven, the skin shining and red, and you can see exactly where the surgeon stitched me back together.

Kingston whistles, soft and low.

"How'd you manage that, sweetheart?"

I twist my leg to show him the worst of it, then roll the fabric back down. As soon as the hem hits my sneakers and I'm covered again, my chest feels a little lighter.

"One of Dad's competitors wanted to send him a message. His men forced our car off the road. It was just me in there, coming back from school, and the car crumpled right around my leg."

My voice is even. I've had eight years to process this, after all. Eight years to work through the nightmares, to get past the flashbacks and the fears of being in a car again.

Maybe Dad should have gone to therapy, too. Then I wouldn't be the only one ready to move on.

I watch Kingston carefully for signs of revulsion or pity. For an excuse to get my hackles up. But while his eyes are sorrowful, he plucks up his cards like we're talking about the weather.

"Don't expect special treatment now, Frankie. I'm still going to rinse you out."

I've got no money to rinse, but he knows that full well. I grin so hard my cheeks ache.

"Bring it. I smashed that interview, and I'll smash this too."

Kingston starts to play, and a pang of sadness hits me out of nowhere. For a moment, I wish Dad could see me the same way Kingston does. As a survivor. Indomitable.

But Dad's not here, and that's just as well, or he'd die of shame at how poorly I play. I forget half the rules as soon we begin, and flagrantly cheat just to make Kingston laugh. It's a beautiful sight—dancing eyes and smooth cheeks—and I ham up my turns worse and worse each time so I can see it over again.

We play and drink and chat until the shadows lengthen on the cobblestones. Then Kingston walks me back to his car, pausing every time the sidewalk is empty to drag me in for a burning kiss.

He doesn't say he misses Jamie. He hasn't lost interest now it's just me.

I love him for that.

I kiss him back with all my might, pouring all of my appreciation and gratitude and my shameless crush against his lips until we're both groaning.

"Let me take you home," he murmurs, and I'm nodding before he's done talking.

"Uhuh. Home. Yes. Let's do this."

He opens the passenger side door to his little red beater, and I slide in like the Queen of Sheba. Riding up front with Kingston is a million times better than hiding behind bulletproof glass in the O'Brien cars.

He fiddles with the radio before we go, frowning until he finds a song to his liking. Then he smiles, warmth spreading over his face, and we pull out into traffic.

* * *

"I thought you meant my dad's estate. Not home, like your home."

I run my finger along the books on Kingston's bookcase, noting all the titles. They're in size and color order, not by author, and most of them are about music in some way. Composers' biographies. Opera librettos. The history of blues.

Kingston's whole apartment is a shrine to music. There are instruments in every room, stacks of sheet music on the coffee table, vinyl records hung on the walls. There's no TV, but a sound system takes up a huge cabinet, and there are speakers on shelves in each corner of the living room. Kingston sets a song playing, something honeyed and low, and opens the glass door to his balcony.

It's swish. I feel like I'm playing a role in a movie when he hands me a glass of wine.

"I figure Jamie will come and throw you over his shoulder at some point," he says, clinking our glasses. "And if not, you can stay for breakfast."

I take a sip and hum. "Works for me."

We stand out on the balcony together, laughing and people watching. And we're on our second glasses of wine when a knock sounds at the door.

Kingston checks his watch. "Your boy's keen."

I shrug, tossing back the rest of my drink. "Paranoid, more like."

But it's not Jamie standing in Kingston's hallway. The door swings open, and I blink.

"You left these on the boat." Gabriel's gruff voice carries through the living room as he hands Kingston a ring of keys. His eyes travel past the younger man's shoulder and widen when they take me in.

I beam at him, excited as a puppy.

"Boss man! Hey!"

Gabriel nods, brows drawing down. Then he turns back to Kingston and mutters something about shifts before turning to leave like he never saw me at all.

Um. What? What happened to the man who propped me up with his chest? Who bequeathed me a uniform shirt so I could remember my first day at work and be proud?

"Hey," I call louder, the wine making me brave. Gabriel looks back, eyebrows raised. "Don't be such an ass, Ortiz. Would it kill you to say hi?"

"Hi," he grits out, but when he turns to go, it's Kingston who grabs his arm.

"What's going on?" He looks between us, confused. I flush bright red at the memory of what happened in Gabriel's office.

"Nothing," I mumble. If he's over it, I'm sure as hell not going to chase after him. Not that Kingston would care—he clearly has a thing for sharing. But I'm not about to admit that I blew two men who'll barely look me in the eye.

And Gabriel must really be out to hurt me, because he mutters, "Nothing important."

Fine. You know what? That about sums it up. I place my wineglass down with a thud on the bookcase. I cross to my bag and rummage for my phone, two sets of eyes burning into my skin.

"What?" I ask dully when I straighten up and they're both looking. Gabriel shifts, his mouth twisting, but I ignore him. I scroll to my top contact and press the phone against my ear.

"Frankie?" Jamie picks up on the first ring. "What is it? What's happened? Are you okay?"

I limp out to the balcony where the others can't hear me, and where the evening shadows can hide my face.

"Will you come and get me?"

"Yes." He doesn't pause to think about it, he just agrees. My heart throbs inside my rib cage. "Where are you?"

I give him Kingston's address, then hang up the phone, scrubbing my cheeks before I limp back inside.

"Thanks for the drink."

I force a bright smile for Kingston, but he doesn't smile back. He frowns at me, concerned, while Gabriel hovers next to him, his face unreadable.

Too bad. I'm so freaking sick of these guys blowing hot and cold. I sling my bag over my shoulder and head for the door.

"I'll let you know about that job, okay?"

"Wait," Kingston says, but the door handle's turning in my hand.

"I call you tomorrow." The door closes with a snap. I take a moment, resting my forehead against the wood, my eyelids drifting closed. Faintly, inside the room, I can hear the sound of raised voices.

Nope. Not my problem. I shuffle away down the hall. The elevator takes an age to arrive, but Gabriel doesn't come out of the apartment.

Works for me. I'm done with putting myself out there only to be trampled on.

* * *

I slide a foam separator between my toes, ignoring my phone as it vibrates on the rug. The kitchen is dark except for the flickering lights of the TV, and the guards cycle past the doorway on their patrols.

Whoopi Goldberg's on screen, telling the world how men ain't shit.

Too right. I hover my hand over a line of nail polish bottles before settling on deep, vicious red.

No sooner has my phone stopped vibrating that it starts all over again, humming and drifting over the rug. I chew on my cheek, contemplating, then flip it over so I can see the screen.

Gabriel's name pops up in an endless list.

Missed call.

Missed call.

Missed call.

Oh, well. I'm sure Gabriel Ortiz, lord of the river, can stand to take a little rejection. He sure knows how to dish it out. The phone stops buzzing and I turn back to my toes.

It's annoying, trying to give yourself the perfect pedicure when your ex boss-slash-hookup won't stop blowing up your phone. I let him go to voicemail four more times before I finally snap and answer the phone, dropping him back to the rug on speaker.

"Take a damn hint, Ortiz."

He has the gall to sound irritated. At me.

"Answer your damn phone and I won't have to keep calling."

"Oh, I didn't realize. Are you at gunpoint?"

He sighs, long and heavy. Like the world is out to give him a hard time. I open my mouth to give him my most colorful insults, but he speaks before I have the chance.

"I'm sorry, Frankie." My mouth shuts with a click. "That's all I wanted to say. I didn't handle seeing you well."

He sounds rueful, his voice rough and tired. Part of me softens, wants to make this all better for him, but then I remember he's been a total ass and harden myself back up.

"Will that be all?"

"It will."

It's like he's answering another question. One that I didn't ask.

"I can't see you again, Frankie."

"I didn't ask you to," I grind out.

"I'm sorry."

"Don't flatter yourself."

We both fall silent, nothing but dead air between us. I blink hard and paint another toe. Long, blood red sweeps of color. The color of my mood.

"You didn't have to be such a prick about it," I whisper at last.

He sighs again, but not like I'm annoying. Like he's tired of himself too, but he can't get away. "What changed, anyway?"

"Nothing changed." I grunt in disbelief, and he corrects himself. "I remembered the nature of the situation."

"What nature? What situation?"

"I'm too old for you," he grits out. "You're a sweet girl, and I'm… we want different things, Frankie."

How can he know what I want if he's never bothered to ask? The last swipe of my nail polish brush is angry, and I stray off the nail. I close my eyes for a second, breathing in hard through my nose, then cap the polish off and unscrew the remover.

"Well, good luck to you," I say dully. I can practically hear him cringe down the phone. "Maybe I'll see you when I visit Kingston sometime."

"That would be nice," he lies. He pauses, dragging this out like he doesn't want to be the one to hang up. Too bad—I've got my hands full here, cleaning up my anger-painting.

"Goodbye, Frankie."

"Bye."

The line drops and I blink hard up at the TV screen. Another guard walks past the kitchen doorway, glancing in to check on me, and I let my hair swing forward to block my face.

They don't get to see this. This is private.

* * *

The sour taste left in my mouth by Gabriel's call lingers until the end of the film. It's late—deep in the early hours—but the thought of going to bed fills me dread.

I haven't been sleeping. Every time I lie there and try to relax, a thousand voices yell at me about the future. I end up staring at the ceiling, or punching my headboard, or scrolling through stupid memes on my phone.

I can't do it. Not another night; not yet. I have to fully exhaust myself before I even try it.

Usually, on nights like these, it'd be Jamie I go to. Even when he's on shift the next day, he always sits up with me and distracts me from whatever is stewing in my brain. We've tried everything to help me sleep—Jamie went through a stage of ordering me 'mindfulness' activities, for example. There's nothing quite so adorable as watching a deadly bodyguard coloring in.

Sometimes he makes me hot chocolate from scratch, with warm milk and melted chocolate. As soon as the thought crosses my mind, my mouth goes dry and my stomach growls.

Hot chocolate, then. How hard can it be? I make coffees all the time.

Forty minutes later, I throw the kitchen windows open and flap a dish towel to get the air moving. The acrid smell of burned milk and charred chocolate lingers in the air, snitching on me to everyone who walks past the doorway.

"Holy shit." As if on cue, Jamie wanders inside, his feet bare on the tiles. He's all sleep-rumpled, his hair sticking up at the back, and his pajama pants look criminally soft. "What happened here?"

I shoot him my sourest look.

"I made a delicious drink."

His mouth ticks up at the corners. "This is the proudest day of my life."

It's my mess, and I fully intend to clean it. But Jamie hums and pads into the kitchen, gathering dishes and pans in the sink.

"I've got that," I tell him.

"It's no problem."

For some reason, that winds my temper another notch tighter.

"I said I've got it. I am perfectly capable of cleaning up my own mess, Jamie."

He frowns at me over his shoulder, already elbow deep in bubbles.

"What's going on?"

I could scream. I could pull my hair out by the roots.

"Who says there's something going on? Why can't I just be in a goddamn bad mood?" I barge him out of the way with my hip and start scrubbing the saucepans like they murdered my family.

Jamie steps to one side, but he stays, watching me.

"You're not sleeping."

"Wow," I bite out, sloshing dishwater onto my feet. "You're so pretty and smart."

"Do you want to talk about it?"

"No."

"Do you want to do something?"

"No."

"I read that knitting—"

"Jamie." I cut him off, my hands stilling. As I turn to him, flecks of foam drift through the air from my frenzy. "I don't want to chat. I don't want to knit, or meditate, or fold little paper cranes. I want to clean these dishes and be furious at everyone."

After a moment, he nods.

"Seems like you've got it covered."

It's a weird feeling as he turns to leave. Half triumph, and half shameful regret. He came in here to check on me, to keep my grumpy ass company if I'd let him, and all I've done in return is bite his head off and slosh dishwater down his sleep pants.

I can't call him back, though. I'm still wound so tight my teeth rattle, furious at the world. Freaking Jamie keeping his noble distance; damn Gabriel doing the same thing by another name. And the man I'm angriest at of all, who lied to me and trapped me and I still miss with each passing day.

A dish slips out of my wet hand and shatters on the kitchen tiles. I pause, waiting for Jamie to charge back in and insist on cleaning up after me.

He doesn't come. I'm both pleased and disappointed as I limp to fetch a broom.

Chapter 9

I wake up on my last day of freedom with a message on my phone.

Gabriel: Meet me on the docks in an hour.

I check the time he sent that message: twenty-seven minutes ago. Then I check my hair: a tangled mess.

Scrubbing the sleep from my eyes, I push up to sit against the headboard and sigh.

I could so easily ignore this. Click my phone off and go back to sleep. It's no less than Gabriel Ortiz deserves. Not to mention that if I want to get there in time, I'll have to rush like the hounds of hell are nipping at my heels.

I press my knuckles into my eyes and groan, long and loud. Then I throw back my bed covers and vault onto the floorboards.

The world's quickest shower, a crumpled pair of jeans and a t-shirt, and a wrestling match with a hairbrush later, and I hustle into the kitchen to find Jamie pacing back and forth by the coffee maker. He stops when he sees me come in, though standing still clearly takes him an effort.

"I need a favor," I begin, but he nods.

"I'll do it."

Damn. That was easy. He doesn't complain when we have to

leave his coffee behind, or when we pull off the driveway and immediately get stuck in traffic. He barely speaks at all, in fact, his eyes staring lifelessly at the road.

I place a fingertip on one of his knuckles as he drums at the steering wheel. He tenses, but stops, his eyes sliding to mine.

"Are you okay?"

He presses his mouth into a line and nods. I withdraw my hand.

The drive takes us too long, and Gabriel's deadline slips by. I chew on my bottom lip, staring out the car window. Jamie didn't even make me sit in the back seat. I've broken him.

The street slides past outside, bright and pale in the morning light. White seabirds drift overhead, riding air currents with their wings outstretched, and when we turn onto the docks road, the river glints like steel.

"Call me when you're done," Jamie mutters, because we both see him at the same time: Gabriel Ortiz, standing with his broad shoulders tensed as he waits for me past his own deadline. He's glowering, wearing a worn plaid shirt and workman's boots, and people skirt around him on the sidewalk.

"Or you could come?"

I make the offer before my brain catches up. Before I remember how I spent the entire week trying to get away from Jamie; how things have soured between us since. But Jamie looks so drawn and exhausted, purple shadows bruising his eyes, and suddenly I want him sealed by my side.

He glances at me, unsure. "You want me there?"

My tongue is thick in my mouth. "Always."

He chews it over, his eyes flicking up to Gabriel waiting in the distance before settling back on me.

"Then I'll come."

* * *

Here's what I thought Gabriel might offer me: a cover shift on the riverboat. Another secret blow job. A brusque but empty apology.

Instead, here's what I got: a long, typed list of names and phone numbers, with their business names below. I frown down at the paper, smoothing it out as the wind tugs at the corners.

"They're in order." Gabriel points at the first name, then over the street at a nearby bar. "We can walk them in a loop and finish back here."

"We?"

Gabriel shoves his hands in his pockets. "I'm your reference, remember?"

Jamie snorts, like he knows exactly what we've been up to.

"I worked an actual shift, you know," I tell him.

He grins and holds up his palms. "I didn't say anything."

He's being an ass, but at least he's smiling. The sight warms my chest, and I straighten an inch.

"Okay." I tug the paper smooth and squint at the first line. "Let's do this."

The first four places we try are a bust. Gabriel's done all he can for me, opening doors and getting me interviews, but he can't magically make me a trained barista or skilled pastry chef. We keep trying, wandering round Gabriel's pre-planned loop, and though my heart sinks a little with every rejection, my steps are lighter than they've been in days. Especially when Jamie slips his hand into mine and squeezes.

I don't let go.

Sometimes, I forget that Dad's only been gone for six days.

That I've known Kingston and Gabriel for less than a week; that the earth shifted under Jamie and me in that time.

It feels like it's always been this way. His hand in mine, and Gabriel or Kingston at our side.

If the older man is put off to see Jamie holding my hand, he doesn't show it. He holds the door open for us at an antique store, the breeze ruffling his dark hair, and I suck in my breath when I squeeze past him.

Jamie raises an eyebrow at me and I poke out my tongue. Damn, he knows me down to my bones.

The store is a cave of oddities. Crystals and dream catchers; embroidered silk scarves; a glass cabinet of animal skeletons. There's a mouse, a crow, and what looks like a fox, their bones threaded onto steel wires. The smell of incense is thick on the air, and a bead curtain rattles as a woman steps through behind the register.

"Greetings," she intones.

I don't have to look at Jamie to know he's biting back a laugh. The woman is draped in long skirts and a shawl, her silvery white hair loose in waves over her shoulders. Gabriel shoots me a stern look as he steps forward, offering his hand.

"Helen." She places her fingers in his palm and he kisses them. I stiffen, not fighting back giggles anymore. "This is Frankie." He jerks his head at me. "The girl I told you about."

I force my lips into a smile and step forward.

"Nice to meet you."

She gives me a sly smile. Her face is powdered white against her shock of plum lipstick, and I can't make out her age. She could be younger than Gabriel, or in her forties too, or decades older for all I can tell.

"Come here, child."

I fight the urge to snap at her and cross to the counter. Beneath the glass are rows of ornate rings and a bowl of mismatched cuff links. Helen holds out her palm, and I reluctantly place my hand in hers. She tuts and flattens my fingers, mouth pursing as she stares at my palm.

Is she for real? I risk a glance at Gabriel, ready to find him creased with laughter, but he shakes his head a fraction.

All right. I blow out a long breath. There must be weirder jobs.

While Helen combs over my life lines, I study her in return. Her hair is matted, any past encounter with a comb a distant memory, but she's clean and her clothes are well made. I'll bet this store draws tourists from far and wide to see the creepy skeletons and the creepier owner.

She glances up at me and winks, and I smile in return.

She's not cracked. She's a smart businesswoman.

"When can you start?" Her voice is brisk, all her earlier breathlessness long gone.

"As soon as you'll have me."

"Any experience?"

Gabriel starts to speak, but I cut him off.

"No. But I'm ready to learn."

She nods, satisfied, and rattles off details of rotas, duties, and pay. I soak it all up, desperate to remember, and pull out my phone to note the most important parts.

Things like my first shift in two days' time. The hourly rate. And the dress code: as creepy as I can be.

Excitement balloons in my chest until it's clawing at my throat. I hold it in until we're back out on the street, far enough away that Helen can't see. Then I whoop, leaping into Gabriel's arms and laughing as he spins me around. He sets me down, smiling wide, and his hands linger on my waist. I crane up towards him, drawn in on a fishing line.

Jamie clears his throat, and something shutters in Gabriel's eyes. He drops his hands and steps back, his face smoothed blank again.

"Congratulations." Jamie tugs me close and kisses my temple, and I fight the urge to jab in the ribs. He couldn't have waited one more minute?

"Good luck, Frankie." Gabriel nods and turns to leave, headed back towards the docks.

"Wait." I snake out a hand and grab his wrist. Jamie bristles next to me, but I ignore him. "I only have one more night. Then..." Then Dad comes back. "Then it's going to be difficult for a while."

Gabriel cocks his head, like he doesn't know what I'm trying to say. I sigh.

"Please don't go just yet."

Understanding dawns in his eyes, along with something like bitterness. Gabriel pauses, eyes flicking to Jamie, then nods.

"All right. Where are we going?"

I slide my grip down his wrist and tangle my fingers in his. He lets me, and though he barely reacts at first, after a second he clenches my hand something fierce. When he looks at Jamie, he tips his chin up in challenge. My bodyguard rolls his eyes, but falls into step on my other side.

"I want to show Jamie your boat."

Gabriel shrugs. "Okay."

"And while we're there, I want to see your office again. Just you and me."

"Ah."

He may insist that we want different things, but his actions tell another story. And I won't push him into anything—I'm not a monster—but I'm laying all my cards out there.

There's a long stretch of silence, and I rub the pad of my thumb over Gabriel's pulse point. I can feel the thrum of his life force under the skin, galloping much faster than his calm face would indicate.

Jamie says nothing. He gazes out over the river, tipping his face into the breeze.

"If you're sure," Gabriel says at last. Like it was his request, and we're the ones doing him a favor. I squeeze his hand, letting him lead us to where his riverboat hunkers on the waves.

It's messy between us, Gabriel and I. With Jamie, too, for that matter. But tonight feels like an ending somehow, and I don't want to spend it away from either of them. I reach out blindly with my spare hand, brushing my knuckles against Jamie's suit jacket. He takes the hint, capturing my hand in his, and the three of us fall into perfect step.

Even when my leg throbs and I slow, they slow with me.

Like it's instinct. Like we're dancing.

* * *

"Watch it!"

Jamie leaps for the baseball, snagging it with the tip of the glove. He whips it back to Gabriel, cocky and grinning, and readies for another throw. I sit on the deck railing, half watching them mess around together, and half watching the sun bleed into the horizon.

The sky flushes pink, and the city lights come on one by one. The old fashioned street lamps on the docks sidewalk flicker on, spreading pools of amber light. I kick my heel against the railing and tip my head back, listening to the suck and slosh of the river water against the hull.

"Frankie!" Jamie yells, then a baseball whizzes past my face and into the waves below. I blink down at the little circle of foam, then up at their grinning faces.

"You bastard!" I hop down off the railing. "You're trying to do me in."

"Can you blame us?" Gabriel calls, his shirt whipping open at the collar. I crack my knuckles like I'm going to fight them both.

Actually… the memory of wrestling with Jamie yesterday, of feeling him pressed up against my body, taking complete control…

Maybe fighting them both at once wouldn't be so terrible after all. I cough to cover the sudden tightness of my throat.

Sidling up to Gabriel, I hook my fingers through his belt loops.

"How about that trip to your office?"

The smile dims on his face, and I know right then that it's happening again. I've misread this, and I'm about to be trampled.

"Frankie…" He unhooks my fingers and clasps my hands in his own. "What happened before… it was wrong of me. A moment of weakness."

I squeeze him back a bit too hard to be friendly.

"Yeah, no kidding. You can just say you don't want me, you know. Don't mess me around like an asshole."

I try to tug my hands free, but he won't let go, and when I look up he's glowering down at me.

"Is that what you think?" He sounds furious. "That I can't make up my mind about whether I want you?"

I shrug. How else am I supposed to read this? But that just makes him even madder. He yanks me towards the steps leading into the boat, never mind what he just said. Jamie starts forward, frowning at Gabriel's rough hold on me, but I shake my head and follow him down into the belly of the beast.

We don't make it to his office. We've barely gone three steps into the top deck bar before Gabriel rounds on me and backs me up against a pool table.

"Is this what you want, Frankie? You won't learn, will you?"

His words shake with anger as he presses up against my front. I arch against him, dying for all the contact I can get, and try to wind my arms around his neck. He catches my wrists, pulling them down and gripping them in one hand behind my back.

I stare up at him, chest heaving, my core impossibly slick. This is nothing like the holds Jamie was training me for. I'd rather scratch out my own eyes than escape right now.

"This is who I am." Gabriel jerks my hands and I whimper. "Rough. Harsh. I'm no match for a sweet young thing like you."

I raise my chin and look him straight in the eyes.

"Try me," I taunt, and roll my hips.

It's like the fine thread holding Gabriel's control in check snaps. He lunges down at me, surrounding, consuming. He kisses me hard enough to bruise; he thrusts a thigh between my legs. His dark eyes glint with satisfaction when I moan and rub myself against him.

Holy shit, I'm going straight to hell, and loving every step of the way. I love the firm grip of his hands; the taste of his tongue as it thrusts into my mouth. I love when he stands back just enough to spin me around and bend me over the pool table. His spare hand makes quick work of my jeans, unbuttoning them and tugging them down my thighs.

The stinging smack on my ass makes me arch my back, gasping up at the porthole window.

On the deck, Jamie leans against the railing, arms crossed as he watches us both. The breeze tugs his suit jacket open, showing a glimpse of his holster against his white shirt.

Gabriel tugs my underwear to the side and runs his thumb over my core.

"Do you like when he watches you?" he growls.

I nod, too worked up to speak. I keep my eyes glued on Jamie, fooling myself that he's staring straight into my eyes in return. And I thrust my hips back against Gabriel, dying for more of his touch.

Another slap stings my ass, and my core floods. I hiss, dropping my forehead onto the cool felt.

"That's it," Gabriel murmurs, rubbing soothing circles on my skin. "Don't think of him right now. Think of me."

It's impossible not to do as he says, not when he slides a finger inside me. His hands are so big that a single finger is enough to stretch me, and I keen and rock back against the table. Gabriel grips my hip in one hand and works me with the other, plunging his finger inside then sliding back out to toy with my clit. I melt over the pool table, boneless and shaking, every touch from him driving me higher.

"Is this what you want, Frankie? To come like this?"

"No." I gasp out the word.

"Tell me what you want. Say the words, sweetheart."

"Your cock. I want your cock."

Gabriel doesn't speak for a moment, and I almost look back, but the crinkle of a foil wrapper settles me back against the felt. I rest my cheek on the table, closing my eyes, all my thoughts focused on the ache between my thighs.

The broad head of Gabriel's cock nudges at my entrance and my heart skips a beat.

"Yes," I breathe, sliding my feet further apart. "Please, Gabriel. I need it."

I don't know who this stranger is, saying these things, but she's more daring than I've ever been. Gabriel curses and slams inside, gripping and spreading my ass cheeks. He sets a brutal rhythm, pounding me against the pool table, and the heavy wooden legs shudder across the floorboards. I moan and push back against him, dying to feel every inch.

Gabriel kicks my feet wider, running a hand up my spine to tangle in my hair. The burn in my scalp when he tugs hard... it's everything. I glance up, eyes wide, and find Jamie closer to the porthole window.

He's not leaning anymore. Not relaxed and casual. Even through the fogged up glass, I can see him vibrating with tension. One hand rests on his holster, the other raking through his hair as he stares at Gabriel working me into a whimpering, boneless mess.

"Enough." Gabriel tugs on my hair, then presses my head down on the felt. "Don't torture the man."

His words are stern, the pump of his hips sharp, but the fingers that slide around my hips to rub at my clit are achingly gentle. That's what breaks me: the soft, careful touch amid the bruising thrust of his cock and the tight grip of his hand in my hair.

I cry out, scrabbling at the pool table and sending the balls clacking against each other. My core clenches down on Gabriel's cock, waves of pleasure shuddering through me, pushed even higher as Gabriel curses and swells inside me. The moment stretches on, both of us tensed and cursing, then we slump down together.

I collapse onto the table, the green felt scratchy against my flushed cheek. I'm sticky and sore, taken apart and put back together all messy, and I wince as Gabriel pulls out of me.

He walks away, footsteps fading across the bar floorboards. Then moments later, he's back, cleaning me up with a warm cloth and easing my jeans back up my thighs.

"You can stand up if you want."

"I don't want," I tell the felt. Gabriel chuckles and coaxes me upright. I wince as I step on my leg, the hot throb singing through the bone.

"Is it bad?" Jamie asks quietly from the doorway. I don't know how long he's been there, watching us, but I shrug, Gabriel's hand a warm weight on my shoulder.

"It's okay."

His mouth tightens, like he knows that I'm lying, or maybe he's just royally pissed about what Gabriel and I just did. Shame tickles at the back of my mind, but I push it away.

No one forced him to watch. And my sex life is none of Jamie's business.

He saw to that.

Suddenly, I'm bone-deep tired. Swaying on my feet. The happy, warm buzz in my veins has made me sleepy, and the way Jamie's looking at me makes me want to crawl into a hole and hibernate. I lean back against Gabriel's chest, savoring the rise and fall of his breath as it rocks me.

"You should get going." His arms wind around me as he says it, barring me from taking his advice. I hum and tip my head back against his collarbone, closing my eyes.

They're back tonight. Mom and Dad. Back from whatever mysterious business drew them to the west coast. I've missed them so much my stomach hurts, but when I think of them coming back, a lump grows in my throat.

I'm not ready. For the rows and the arguments; for the sheer effort of taking a stand. I've spent eight years playing the dutiful daughter, and I'm not so sure I'm good for anything else.

"Come on." Jamie takes my hand and pulls me out of Gabriel's hold. "Time to stop hiding, Frankie."

I turn to say goodbye to Gabriel, and his mouth stretches into a rare smile. He tucks a strand of hair behind my ear, fingertips lingering on my neck.

Then: "Be good." He drops a kiss onto my forehead. I close my eyes, savoring the press of warmth.

Jamie says nothing as we cross the bar, though he walks slower than usual on account of my limp. He stays silent all the way down the stairs and off the riverboat into the street.

The evening breeze washes over my skin, cooling my lingering blush. I risk a glance at Jamie and find his face blank as stone, though his hand is still tight around mine.

I swallow and limp after him to the car.

Time to face my father.

Chapter 10

The lights are off at the estate, except for the driveway and security guard's hut. A single lamp shines in the window of the guards' office, just off the living room, and the light of a TV screen flickers against the wall, but no one's really home yet.

Good. Better that we get home first and ease Dad into it.

He definitely knows I've been going out. And possibly knows about my night with Kingston and Jamie. That shame tickles at my brain again, but I push it away more forcefully this time.

I've done nothing wrong. Nothing to be ashamed about. I've been a brat to Jamie a couple of times, sure, but wanting my own life—wanting to see the city, to get a job, to explore my sexuality—that is not a sin. I'm an adult, for God's sake. I straighten my spine and march through the front door.

Jamie heads straight for the kitchen, pulling a bottle of whiskey out of the cupboard. He pours himself two fingers' worth, knocking it back and slamming his glass down on the counter. I follow after him, watching carefully as my calm, ruthless bodyguard unravels at the seams.

His red hair sticks up, disheveled from his hands, and he shrugs his suit jacket off and tosses it on a stool. It lands, then slithers off to land in a heap on the tiles. Jamie watches, then turns away.

"Are you okay?"

Even though I speak quietly, it's still deafening in the cold, empty room. Jamie jerks his head at me, like he's annoyed I'm even here.

"Of course I'm okay."

"Only you seem kind of rattled."

"I'm fine."

The kitchen tap drips.

"It's just, on the boat—"

"I said I'm fine, Francesca."

I fall silent, hovering awkwardly next to the breakfast bar as Jamie pours himself another drink. He sips this one, grimacing even as he sighs with relief, then sets it back on the counter.

Seriously. What is the point of whiskey?

"If what happened with Gabriel bothers you—"

Jamie rounds on me. "And why would it bother me, hm? Are you so determined to make me jealous? Because it won't work, Francesca. I don't care what you do."

My face flushes hot as he speaks, but I grip the counter and stay rooted to the spot.

"You're being such an asshole."

"Am I?" Jamie steps closer, eyes bright. "But you like that, don't you?"

"Not from you."

Never from him. Not the man who kept me company for eight long years, who brought me magazines and sat up with me when I was sick. Who looks at me now like he doesn't know me at all, just because I had sex with someone I like. Someone I care about.

"You didn't care when Kingston was here and we—"

"Don't say it." Jamie points at me. "I'm warning you, Frankie."

"Or what?" I limp around the counter, because that's the biggest load of crap I've ever heard. Jamie would cut his own hand off before he hurt me. "It happened, Jamie. You can't take it back."

"It did not!" he roars, and I stumble back. I'm not scared, just surprised, but my back hits the counter at a funny angle and I grunt in pain. Jamie's face tightens, drains deathly white, and he reaches for me before snatching his hand back and turning on his heel.

He's out of the room before I can tell him to stay.

I toss back the rest of his whiskey then slam the glass on the counter. It burns all the way down.

* * *

After the third lap of my bedroom, I'm resolved. Mom and Dad still aren't home, and we have God knows how long to fix this. To talk freely, openly, without ears everywhere. Jamie may want to hide from me and sulk, but I won't spend my last night with him like this.

Not barricaded away in different parts of the house, nursing hurt feelings and a boatload of regrets.

I stride out into the hallway, burning with righteous purpose. I don't falter until I find his quarters empty.

So is the kitchen. And the living room. There's no sign of him in the guards' office either.

"Um." A middle aged man with a shiny bald spot glances up at me from their table. Two of them are playing cards, the bank of monitors forgotten over their shoulders. If Dad finds them slacking like this, they'll be tossed on the street. "Is Jamie around?"

The man gives me a knowing smirk and jerks his head at the monitors.

"Check the gardens."

I wander over to the screens, frowning at the flickering images of the grounds.

The ponds are empty, the tumbling streams of the water fountains fuzzing like static on the screen. The back porch is the same: the decking clear except for the empty benches and potted shrubs. I glance back over my shoulder, but the guards are deep in their game.

Fine. He must be here somewhere. It can't be that easy for a six-foot-three bodyguard in a suit to hide.

There: a shoulder pokes out from behind a column in the gazebo. Even that scrap of him, I know by heart. I force a smile for the guards and limp back into the hallway.

The walk to the gazebo takes me ten minutes. Ten minutes to rehearse what I want to say; for nerves to build up and churn in my stomach. But when I see him—sitting on the wooden railing, one knee pulled up as he leans back against the wood—all that flies out of my brain.

"Jamie," I call, limping faster. He glances over at where I'm forging down the garden path, his own face etched with sorrow.

We don't say anything. We don't need to. He slides down off the railing just as I reach him, launching into his arms. He catches me, burying his face in my neck, and we hold each other tight enough to mold into one.

"I'm sorry. I'm so sorry, Frankie."

I shake my head, tears brimming in my eyes. I set out to build myself a new life this week, but I wound up demolishing the most precious thing I have.

"Please don't hate me, Jamie. I can't bear it."

He pushes me back by the shoulders, ducking his head to glare into my eyes.

"I could never hate you, Frankie. Never. Not as long as I live."

His blue eyes are so fierce, so sure of his words, and it should help. Should soothe the pain in my chest. But all it does is make my face crumple and tightens my throat.

Strong arms bind around me, pulling me against his chest, and I suck in deep lungfuls of Jamie. As I breathe out, a hiccup turns into a sob, and he gathers me impossibly closer.

"What's this about, beautiful girl?"

I cry harder. What is there to say? *I'm in love with you and you don't want me back?*

"Is this about your father?"

I shake my head.

His voice hardens. "About your other men?"

I clutch at his shirt, pressing my face against the sliver of bare skin showing between his open top buttons.

"Do you hate me for it?"

He laughs, the sound harsh, but he doesn't push me away.

"No, Frankie. If anything, I like it a bit too much."

I draw back, confused, and frown at the blush tinting his cheeks. He licks his lips and stares over my shoulder.

"You… want me, then?"

He sighs. "It's not as simple as that."

"Why not?" I speak louder. "Why can't it be?"

"Because of Carrick. Because of everything I owe him. And because you deserve someone good, and gentle, like Kingston." His face clouds over. "I'm not sure about this latest one, mind. He's too firm with you."

I ignore that last part and shake Jamie by the shirt, or at least I go through the motions. He's not a very movable man.

"You're good. You're gentle."

My heart breaks when he looks down at me, something broken behind his eyes.

"I'm neither of those things, Francesca."

"You are with me."

He opens his mouth to argue, but I don't give him the chance. I rise on my toes and kiss him, nice and gentle like he's talking about. I pour everything into that kiss: all those years of wanting him so badly. Of lying in my bed at night, unable to sleep, every inch of my body crying out for Jamie.

It takes a moment that feels a thousand years long, but then he kisses me back, lips moving against me.

We've done this before, the night with Kingston, but not like this. Not flayed open and alone with each other.

"You really don't mind about the others?" I ask when we pull apart to breathe. My heart climbs into my throat while I wait for him to answer.

It's not the same with Gabriel and Kingston as it is with Jamie and I. It couldn't be—we've only known each other for a week. But something tells me, down deep in my soul, that I need them both too.

That the four of us are meant for each other, and without them, this will all fall apart.

After all, Jamie and I went years without saying anything to each other. And when I finally told him what I wanted, it still wasn't enough.

Kingston coaxes him out, draws Jamie to join us with soft words and smooth kisses.

Gabriel dares him to step up to the challenge.

Without them, the weight of Jamie's debt to my family pulls him under. Locks him away where I can't reach.

"No," he says at last. "I don't mind sharing you. So long as I keep a piece of your heart."

I give a wobbly smile, my cheeks still wet from tears, and kiss him again, sweet and slow.

"Always. I promise."

"I'll hold you to that."

I wind my arms around his neck. "Don't you want to stake another type of claim?"

Jamie's eyes darken, a thrill shooting down my spine, then he scoops me up in his arms the same way he carried me to his bedroom with Kingston.

"You'd better not walk all the way back to the house." I nip at his earlobe.

His laugh rumbles through his chest. "Just away from the cameras."

He chooses a stone bench a short way down the path, shrubs and hedges climbing high on all sides. When he lowers himself down, I plant my knees on either side of his hips, shuffling closer until we're aligned.

"Answer me this honestly: did you take the gardener's lads back here?"

I cock my head. "On this specific bench?"

He grins and swats my ass, and I grind down against him, tilting my head back when he kisses up my throat.

"I knew it." He scrapes his teeth over my skin.

"That's because I wanted you to know."

He hums and swats me again.

It's not hard and fast, like with Gabriel, nor soft and slow like with Kingston. Jamie's always been a delicious mix in between. He takes me apart, undressing me, touching me everywhere—unhurried, like we have all the time in the world.

And he brings me to climax again and again, like he won't be happy until he holds the record. First with his fingers, rubbing solely at my clit, then again when he slides two digits inside me. He takes me apart until I'm aching and needy, and only then does he fish a condom out of his pocket.

"Frankie," he breathes as I sink down onto his length. I nod, wordless, and rest my forehead against his.

We rock together, sealed tight and clinging, our breaths the only sound in the gardens except for the breeze whispering through the leaves. The scent of jasmine drifts over us as the last rays of light drain from the sky, pinpricks of starlight shining overhead.

"I love you," I tell him, voice hoarse, as the tension builds in my core. It gathers slow and steady, like a thunderstorm, all the more powerful for our patience.

"You're everything," he mutters against my skin. "My heart and soul." I shatter, crying out as tears blur my eyes, and he follow me with a curse.

I never want to get up. Never want to untangle our limbs and right our clothes and pat down our sex-wild hair. But headlights swoop down the estate driveway, the beam filtering through the surrounding shrubs, and reality slides back in, cold and harsh.

"It'll be right, Frankie." He tucks my hair behind my ear and presses a kiss to my nose. "You'll see."

I nod, legs shaking as I climb off his lap. The breeze is cool as it skates over my bare skin, goosebumps erupting over my limbs.

"Right. Okay, yeah." I tug my jeans on, mouth twisting as I

stare across the grounds at the house.

Dad is home.

* * *

Most parents would probably be thrilled to hear their grown daughter plans to move out. To hear she has a new job and is in love with a good man.

Maybe most parents wouldn't be thrilled about their daughters collecting a harem, but that's besides the point.

Mom and Dad are not most parents.

We get back to the house in time to meet them in the lobby, dropping their suitcases on the tiles and shrugging off their coats. Dad breaks into a huge smile as soon as he sees me, showcasing the crooked tooth he refuses to get fixed.

"Frankie! How was your week, sweet girl?"

He opens his arms and I walk into them without hesitation, squeezing him and breathing in the smell of his cologne.

I'm so mad at him, yet I've missed him so much. I squeeze harder, until I can feel his heartbeat thrumming in his chest.

"Don't think you're not royally in trouble," he murmurs into the crown of my head—and there's the issue. To Carrick O'Brien, I'm still the fourteen year old girl who got injured in his place. A child in need of rules and protection.

I give a sharp nod and step out of his arms. He watches me, gray eyes calculating.

"About that. Dad—"

"And what am I, chopped liver?"

Mom throws her hands up where she's draped over the banister. Even after a full day of travel, she's spotless—not a platinum hair out of place. If I'd just arrived home from the airport, I'd be sweaty and in dire need of a shower. Not Mom.

"Sorry." I grin and limp over to her, pulling her far enough upright to hug her too. She winds her arms around me, the touch barely there, and I squeeze her tighter to compensate.

"Oof. All right, don't crease my blouse, Francesca."

I roll my eyes and let her go.

"Missed you too, Mom."

Jamie hovers in the background, a crackling ball of tension in the corner of the lobby. Mom doesn't even acknowledge his presence—she's always been somewhat cold with him—but Dad stares outright, his dark gaze flicking between the two of us.

There's not much time, now. It's all coming out, one way or another.

"Drink?" Dad asks, clapping his hands together and rubbing them. He strides towards the door to the kitchen, but neither Jamie nor I move.

"Um. Wait a second, Dad."

He pauses, turning his head back to watch me over his shoulder. The light from the kitchen casts stark shadows across his face in the dim lobby.

"Don't tell me just yet, Frankie, love. I want a drink in my hand."

That sounds like a terrible addition to this scenario, but I nod and follow him anyway. Jamie lingers, and for a sickly second I think he's going to make me do this alone. But then Mom floats through the door after Dad, her narrow shoulders slumped, and Jamie pushes away from the wall.

He crosses to me, wrapping his fingers around my wrist and rubbing his thumb over my pulse point.

"It'll be okay, Frankie." His voice is low, his words just for me. I blow out a breath and nod, steeling my spine.

"Why am I so scared of what they think? It's none of their business, really."

Jamie shrugs. "You love them."

They're not the only ones I love.

True to his word, Dad stands at the counter, pouring whiskey into a cut-glass tumbler. Mom is strewn over the couch, plucking at a loose thread on a cushion. Both heads turn to me as I limp through the doorway, narrowing my eyes against the sudden bright lights.

"Dad. Both of you. I need to tell you something."

Dad hums, knocking back a gulp of his drink then setting it on the counter. He lets out a guttural sigh, rolling his neck, and gives me a wry glance.

"What shall we start with? Your day trips? Your new job? Or your three boyfriends?"

For the first time since coming home, he looks straight at Jamie, eyes hard, a nerve leaping in his jaw. Even without turning my head, I feel my bodyguard flinch behind me.

I'm not the only one who cares deeply what Carrick O'Brien thinks.

"Don't look at him like that." Dad's eyes snap back to me, and I raise my chin. "Jamie's done nothing wrong. Neither have I."

Dad scoffs. "You mean besides proving himself the worst bodyguard on my payroll?"

Again, I feel the man who made a second family with us cringing behind me.

"He did just fine. Annoyingly well. I'm the one who kept sneaking away from him, Dad."

Jamie clears his throat, stepping up to my side. "Carrick," he begins, but Dad raises a palm and cuts him off.

"You're out, lad. I don't take chances with my daughter. I'll give you a day to pack up your things."

If I strain, I'm sure I could hear Jamie's heart break. His face drains of color, his skin turning ashen, and when I clasp his hand in mine, his grip is weak.

"Fine." I glare at the man pouring himself another drink. "He'll move in with me."

Dad snorts. "He will not."

"I'm not asking."

"Doesn't matter. This is my house."

"I don't mean here!"

I take a deep breath, my heart hammering as I watch realization dawn on my father's face. I guess whichever guard's been telling tales forgot to mention our apartment hunt. He rounds the counter, steps clumsy, and walks towards us.

"No." He points at Jamie, two angry spots of color glowing on his cheeks. "No. You'll not have her."

"Carrick," Jamie says, voice hollow. "Please."

"No!" Dad draws level with us, and his eyes shine with manic light as he points between us, finger shaking. "This stops now. You've proven you can't keep her safe. That means there's no space for her in your life."

"That's not your call." I bat his finger away, chest heaving with anger. "I'm going, Dad, and if you make me choose between you and Jamie, I promise you won't come out on top."

There's an audible gasp from the sofa, and Dad freezes, eyes wide. I squeeze Jamie's hand, my palm clammy against his. Then Dad crumples, his face collapsing, and he has never looked so old or so sad.

"Frankie," he whispers. "Don't do this to your old man."

My chin wobbles, and all I want to do is rush into his arms

and take it all back. But I force myself to stay put, anchored by Jamie's hand, and look him straight in the eye.

"I'm going. Jamie's coming with me. You'll be more than welcome to visit, just as soon as you start respecting my decisions."

His shoulders curl, his mouth pressed in a tight line, and I decide I'm done for the night. We can all go to bed, take a few hours to cool down, and try this again in the morning.

I'm leaving either way, but I'd rather not cut every tie in the process.

"Come on." I tug on Jamie's hand. "We can talk more tomorrow." I turn to go, leg throbbing like I've been running, not arguing.

Jamie stays put, hand reaching out for Dad.

"Carrick. I tried to keep away from her, I swear—"

Dad's fist thuds against Jamie's cheek, his head snapping back.

"You didn't try very fucking hard, did you?" Dad bellows as Jamie staggers back, hand clapped to his face.

He looks at me, panic and loss warring on his face.

Then he turns and plunges out of the doorway, out into the shadows.

Chapter 11

I've never been so pissed with myself for not learning to drive. Oh, I asked for lessons of course, the minute I turned old enough. But I ate up Dad's excuses about my leg and the dangers without a second thought.

It's always Jamie who drives me everywhere. And now he's gone, peeling down the driveway in one of Dad's cars.

I will never forgive you for this. That's what I told my wide-eyed father, limping away from him without another word. And it's true: if he's done too much damage, if Jamie doesn't come back, I will blame my father for the rest of his life.

A faded red beater pulls up at the curb as I march down the sidewalk towards the city. The window rolls down and Kingston leans out, calling my name as he slows to a stop.

The knot in my chest eases a fraction of an inch, and I rush to the passenger door. Flinging it open, I slide into the car and promptly burst into tears.

"Easy, now." Kingston buckles me in, squeezing my knee before putting the car back in drive. "We'll find your boy."

I cry harder, too wound up by such a long, messy day that I can hardly see straight. Was it really just hours ago that Jamie and Gabriel were laughing and tossing a baseball back and forth on the riverboat deck?

The memory is like a movie reel. Someone else's life. I sniff hard and scrub my cheeks with my sleeve, pulling the scraps of myself back together.

Jamie. We need to find Jamie. He looked so broken as he left.

"Where does he like to go?" Kingston glances in his mirror, merging with the line of headlights headed towards the city.

I wrack my brain, but the truth is, I don't know where Jamie goes when he's not with me. Because even on his days off, even when he wasn't on duty, he's always come to my side. I used to think it was a pity thing—that he knew how lonely I got sometimes in that house.

I know better now. We've always been as lonely as each other.

Kingston's waiting for an answer, but I don't have one. I shrug, twisting my fingers in my lap.

"I don't know. He's—he's always with me."

Kingston squeezes my knee again, mouth pursed as he stares out the windshield. I breathe in deep and take a moment to appreciate the man who dropped everything, who called out of a shift to race across the city as soon as I told him I needed him.

"Thank you," I whisper.

He gives me a soft look.

"Oh, sweetheart. You don't have to thank me for this."

Either way, I could kiss him right now. I draw my feet up on the seat instead, resting my chin on my knees.

"Why is your apartment so nice but your car's so..." I trail off, hearing how rude I sound. But Kingston chuckles, not offended.

"I traded cars with my Mama. I know how to fix this one when it breaks, anyway."

I picture him with his sleeves rolled up, bent over the hood of a car. Muscles flexing, sweat glistening. It's the sweetest sort of distraction.

"I fixed a bike chain once," I offer. "Back when I could ride."

"Are you sure you can't ride now?"

I chew on my lip, considering. "Huh. I'm not sure."

So many things to try. Different paths to go down. And I want Jamie there for all of them.

* * *

With every street we drive down, every bar we duck inside, I lose a shred of hope. The city is massive, a sprawling beast curled around the river, and it would take weeks to search it properly. Never mind that we could be close, be within meters of Jamie, and look the wrong way at the wrong moment.

I see now why he tracked my phone. I'd give anything to pull up a little red dot on a screen and let it lead me to Jamie.

To Kingston's eternal credit, he never complains. Never suggests that it's time to give up on this wild goose chase. He drives me for hours, even stopping to refuel, then holds my hand as we check inside dozens of bars.

There are so many damn people—so many freaking redheads—that I think I've found him hundreds of times before the night's over. Then I grab their shoulders, or they turn to speak to someone, and their profile's all wrong. It's not him.

We slump against the hood of Kingston's car, gazing up at the glowing signs of bars and restaurants. My feet are blistered in my sneakers, my leg aching something fierce, and we're no closer to finding him now than we were six hours ago.

I bow my head. I'm the first to say it. I'm pretty sure Kingston would keep me company all night if I wanted.

"Okay. I guess, um. I guess he doesn't want to be found."

A warm weight settles over my shoulders, and Kingston draws me close.

"We'll look again tomorrow," he says into my hair. I check my phone for the millionth time: nothing. I switch it off and on again, just in case there's a message from Jamie floating somewhere in the ether. The message icon blinks back at me, cursedly empty.

I'm not sure I could step foot in my father's house without burning it down, so I don't resist when Kingston offers to take me to his apartment. I couldn't leave him if I wanted to right now—his arm around my shoulders is all that's holding me together.

It's a short drive, and he passes me his phone as we go.

"You hungry?"

I rasp out a yes.

"Me too. Order us a pizza."

Melted, cheesy goodness sounds exactly like what I need. Hell, part of me wants to order a family sized pizza then curl up in it like a sleeping bag. I thumb through the app, reading out toppings and cringing when we get to the payment screen.

I left my money at the estate. I don't even have my own bank account yet. But Kingston glances over and clicks his tongue, urging me to put it on his card.

Tears brim in my eyes for the millionth time today, and I place the order.

I'll make it up to him. I'll pay back every cent. And one day, when Kingston has a crisis, I'll be the one person he knows he can call. His phone buzzes in my hand and I give it back without looking, turning to stare out the window. I'm so tired the city lights blur into colored lines: yellow, crimson, blue.

"Nearly there," he tells me, and I mutter something in response. And when we pull up at the curb, I fumble with my seat belt as Kingston rounds the car to open my door.

"I'm not completely helpless," I mumble, even as I grip his hand tight to scramble out the car.

"Never thought you were."

I glance around hopefully as we cross the street, but there's no flash of red hair. No crisp white shirts. I sigh and follow Kingston inside, Jamie's name thudding inside me with every beat of my pulse.

* * *

Each step up to Kingston's apartment is a fight. A fight against my throbbing leg and my tired muscles and the sheer weight of my exhaustion. My breath saws in and out of my chest, my lungs working overtime, and when Kingston pushes his apartment door open, I can't breathe for a different reason.

Gabriel surges to his feet from the sofa, crossing to me in the doorway before I can process what I'm seeing.

"Sweet girl."

He gathers me into his arms and I blink stupidly at the chest hairs poking through his open collar. His shirt is thick and warm, the opposite of Jamie's perfectly pressed suits, and I bury my nose in the fabric.

"What are you doing here?" I ask, voice muffled.

"Kingston texted me. He told me what happened with your man."

A breath shudders out of me, and Gabriel gathers me closer. A large palm lands softly on my head, smoothing down the back of my hair.

This is... unexpected. We had sex, yes—sex so hot my toes curl just to think about it—but Gabriel has always been untouchable, somehow. Aloof. Unaffected.

He's not unaffected now. He draws me to the sofa and bundles me onto his lap, wrapping a tartan throw around me. Kingston gives me a small smile and wanders to the kitchen, the clink of coffee mugs floating through the apartment.

"There was no sign." He's stating a fact, not asking a question. If we knew where Jamie was right now, no force on this earth could keep me away.

"No. He—he just needs to cool down." I try to sound more certain than I feel, to squash the doubts churning in my stomach.

Dad kicked him out. Turned him away from the only real home he's known. And ever since Jamie roared away down that driveway, the same question has been drumming in my brain: *Was I worth it?*

Gabriel hums and rearranges me, tucking my head under his chin. I feel the bob of his throat when he swallows; can breathe his scent in with each draw of my lungs. Something hot and uncomfortable spreads through my chest, and I let my eyes drift closed.

"I took off once," Gabriel says out of nowhere. His low voice rumbles through his chest. "After my brother died. No one could reach me for three weeks. I missed his funeral."

"I'm sorry," I whisper, eyes still shut. "What... what happened to him?"

"He drowned." The riverboat rises up in my mind's eye, but he answers the question before I ask it. "He was at a beach down the coast. A little kid got in trouble in the currents, and Rafael saved his life. But the water took him instead."

I wonder if it's hard for Gabriel on the river. To see the waves lapping against the docks; to hear the suck of water against the hull of his boat. Whether it's a constant reminder, and if it is, whether it's a sweet one.

"I'm sorry," I whisper again. Gabriel rubs his chin in my hair, his stubble catching on the strands.

"I couldn't face it. Couldn't process it all. So I took off and left my family hanging." His hand lands on my knee, heavy and warm, then slides down and kneads my calf. "I was so ashamed. But, you know, sometimes people need that space. It doesn't mean they're not coming back."

I swallow hard. "I did this to him."

"No, Frankie." He kisses my temple. "This is life."

His touch is so different from hours ago. Soft and measured where earlier he was deliciously firm. Weirdly, both make me feel cherished. Safe in his arms; under his grip. And when Kingston brings us mugs of peppermint tea, steam curling over the rim, I gather it into my hands and clutch the burning heat to my chest.

"The food will be here soon." Kingston drops a kiss to the crown of my head, then shares a look with Gabriel over my shoulder. I don't think there's anything there, not like with him and Jamie, but there's a kinship built on years of understanding.

"Thank you." I wriggle on Gabriel's lap, leaning back on his chest as I look up at Kingston. "Both of you. Thank you for this."

"Any time, sweetheart," is all Kingston says, and Gabriel hums in agreement.

I sip my tea, sweet warmth spreading over my tongue.

They stay up with me, taking turns to hold me, and eventually merging into one big tangle on the sofa. They stay awake, even when their jaws crack from yawning, all because of the knot of anxiety in my chest which makes sleep impossible. And we drink tea, and tell each other confessions in hoarse, hushed voices.

Kingston puts music on, soft enough that we won't wake the neighbors.

We open the balcony door to let in a breeze.

And I grip my phone so tight that my knuckles creak, waiting for Jamie to tell me he's okay.

* * *

The morning dawns dull and gray, the sky like dirty dishwater. I take a scalding shower in Kingston's bathroom, staying under the spray for far too long and sniffing his shampoo and body wash. The hot water beats against my back, warming me from the outside in and scouring away some of the exhaustion of the night.

I'm so damn tired. My vision keeps blurring at the edges, and the kernel of a tension headache is throbbing behind my right eye.

But it's a new day. The fresh start I've been building towards.

I can't control Jamie. Can't force him to come home and stay with me. Just like I can't force Mom and Dad to approve of my life choices. To let me leave their house and be my own person.

I loose a long breath and let those things go.

I try to, anyway. I'm only human. And if the loss of Jamie is still a yawning hole in my chest, at least I'm not deliberately wallowing in it. No—there's too much to do. Too many things I can control. Like moving out of the O'Brien estate.

Tessa answered my tentative message first thing this morning. There's a room for me in her apartment if I want it, and I can move in any time. And she followed that God-sent text up with about a million mismatched emojis.

Time to take control. Do this life thing for real. And I just so happen to have my own moving crew.

"Are you sure you don't mind?" I ask them both for the third time, sitting cross legged in front of Kingston's coffee table. The French toast and fresh coffees he made us send little curls of steam into the air. When I dig in, taking a huge bite, my eyes cross. It tastes so good.

"Shut up, Frankie," Gabriel says mildly, flicking through a photography magazine. "We've already told you we're helping." His face is pale, the shadows under his eyes darker from his sleepless night, but he winks at me when he catches me staring.

I look at Kingston instead, chewing on my French toast, and he smiles, cheek dimpling.

"It'll be fun. I need a workout anyway."

The mouthwatering cut of his shoulders would imply otherwise, but I'm not about to complain. In truth, I'd figure the moving part out one way or another—hire a crew or an Uber and do it myself. But while I'm standing a little taller this morning, the last thing I feel like doing is facing down my family alone.

Back up. That's what I need. Strong, sexy back up who, with any luck, will give my father a coronary.

It's such an uncharitable thought, and I send up an immediate prayer to undo it. I want Dad to back off and feel a healthy dollop of shame for how he's treated Jamie. I don't want him to die.

Still, if anything will tip him over the edge, it'll be the sight of my much older boyfriend.

We pile into Gabriel's truck instead of Kingston's old beater. It's just like Gabriel: sturdy and masculine, cocooning you in safety the second you slide into a seat. I suddenly have a burning urge to see where this mysterious man lives.

In a city apartment? A house out in the hills? In a lair in the nearby caves?

I don't ask. I've always hated spoilers. I want to receive the pieces of Gabriel in the order he chooses to dole them out.

But my money's on a secret cavern. Just saying.

Gabriel takes the docks route, probably out of habit. I roll my window down, breathing in lungfuls of freshwater breeze, and listen to the seabirds shrieking overhead. The tears of last night have scoured me clean, and my head feels clear for the first time in days.

Like Jamie keeps telling me. It'll be right.

There are lines of cars along the riverfront, idling as cautious drivers nudge into parking spaces. The cafes are opening, their owners setting out chairs and wiping down tables, and street vendors push carts along the sidewalk.

"Son of a..."

I glance at Gabriel. He leans over the steering wheel, craning his neck as we draw near to his boat.

"What? What is it?" I scrabble for the controls, winding my window down. The morning heat washes over my skin as I stick my head out the window, gazing up at the boat.

I don't see it. The riverboat seems fine, bobbing in the waves against the dock. I squint, tracking my gaze past all the windows, looking for some kind of trouble.

Nothing.

"What are you..." I begin to ask, but then I see it. See him.

The flash of red hair on the top deck—a man in a suit, sat

on the railing. I suck in a sharp breath, my ears ringing, and start babbling at Gabriel to pull over, damn it, or we'll lose him again. Kingston's hand snakes between the seats and squeezes my shoulder, and I sit back, heart pounding.

"Relax, sweetheart," he whispers, velvet in my ear. "If he's up there, your boy wants to be found."

They're wise words, but when Gabriel slows to another halt, I unclip my seat belt and throw my car door open. Gabriel calls after me, exasperated, and Kingston whoops as I lunge out onto the sidewalk. I slam the door behind me and set off, barely limping as I rush towards the boat.

The ramp is down, laid out like a welcome mat. I wobble up it, ignoring the hungry waves, and step on board. My feet lead me on autopilot, winding through halls and up flights of steps, until I spill out onto the top deck.

Jamie sits on the railing, directly opposite the stairwell. He's not surprised to see me. He raises a hand, smiling ruefully.

I choke back every curse, every manic demand that he explain himself, and step forward.

"Are you… all right?"

He doesn't reply. Doesn't nod or shake his head. Just slides off the railing to stand.

More than anything, I want to charge at him and tackle him into a hug. But pushing him is part of what got us here, and I don't want to mess this up. Not with Jamie.

He raises his eyebrows when he sees I'm hanging back, shoving his hands in his pockets and strolling forwards.

"I thought you'd have all sorts of names to call me."

I huff. "I'm calling you them in my head."

"Very restrained."

"I'm working on it."

A shadow passes over Jamie's face, but then he stops and looks out towards the sun. "Your father wouldn't hold back," he murmurs.

I chance another step forward. Then another, until he's almost in arm's reach.

"Forget him. He's not your family." Hurt tightens Jamie's eyes, still staring out over the waves, but I keep talking. "I am, though. If you want me to be."

He looks at me at last, a wry smile tugging his mouth.

"Depends on the relation, I suppose. Are we talking weird cousin or wife?"

Wife? I splutter, choking on my own tongue, and Jamie throws back his head and laughs, a rich, happy sound.

"Maybe one day, then."

"Way in the future," I wheeze. He grins and takes hold of my shoulders.

"That wasn't a no, Francesca."

I wind my arms around him while I have the chance, gripping his shirt at his back like that will stop him from slipping away again. He hugs me back, tight and warm, and speaks into my hair.

"I'm sorry for running."

I nod, my nose pressed against his throat. "Pretty rude since I can't exactly chase you."

"That's what your spare boyfriends are for."

"Among other things," a deep, husky voice rings out, and Gabriel emerges from the stairwell behind me. He strolls towards us, somehow both relaxed and stern. "Break onto my boat again and I'll toss you overboard."

Kingston snorts as he joins us on the deck.

"All right, Blackbeard." He ruffles Jamie's hair. "Hello,

sweetheart."

I pull back to grin at the blush creeping over Jamie's cheeks. Ah, redheads.

"We're going to move me out of the estate."

"We could move you too," Kingston offers.

Jamie clenches his jaw, staring out over the waves again, then his shoulders slump.

"All right. Thank you."

This is so much worse for him. I'm leaving by choice; he's been turned away from his home. We've got something good here, though, between the four of us. You can see it in the way Gabriel claps Jamie on the shoulder, the way we fall into perfect step. He won't have to look far to find somewhere he belongs.

I nudge him with my elbow as we walk.

"Maybe you could work in the store with me."

Gabriel chuckles as Jamie glares at me, rankled.

"I'm a trained bodyguard, Francesca. I've killed men."

"See?" I point at him. "Helen would love that shit."

We file down into the boat one by one, our voices bouncing around the stairwell.

Chapter 12

ONE YEAR LATER

The parade is huge this year. Kingston says it gets bigger, brighter, more raucous with each passing year—the costumes more outrageous, the music louder, the street food sizzling and spicy. I lean on the store counter, watching the crowds surge along the sidewalk by the window. Our display is done up for the parade, covered in feathers and sparkly beads. I even wound little feather boas around the animal skeletons.

It's... a lot. I'm not too sad to be tucked away in the store, away from the chaos for a few minutes longer. This time last year, I ran from Jamie in the car and just about passed out from the onslaught of sensations.

I'll go out there soon. I'm much harder to stress these days. But first, I have something to take care of.

I smooth my palms down the front of my corset, laced over the top of a billowing lilac shirt. *Look the part,* Helen always says, and it's kind of a fun challenge trying to one-up myself with outfits for work.

Kingston's gotten into it too, picking me up weird shirts and dresses when he sees them in thrift stores. He bought me these boots—flat, motorcycle style, studded with tiny metal skulls. They're Helen-approved.

I round the edge of the counter, pausing to tidy up a table of antique jewelry boxes. Dad still cringes whenever he talks about me being a retail worker, but it's more than he thinks. It's creativity. Business decisions. And one day, when I've learned enough here, I'll open my own store.

Besides, he can't talk. At least I'm on the straight and narrow. Even when Carrick O'Brien cleans up his act, he's still one foot in the shadows.

The shop bell tinkles, and a man steps through the doorway, shoulders too broad for this tiny room.

"Finishing up?"

I smirk at Gabriel Ortiz.

"Don't bullshit me. I know you're in here to hide from the crowds."

He shrugs, unabashed, and wanders to the display cabinets, the floorboards creaking under his weight. You'd think he'd be crashing into things, knocking over fragile antiques, but he's surprisingly graceful. Precise and powerful. Like a big cat.

The memory of his strong, feline form stretched over me last night makes me shiver.

"I won't be long," I say, voice husky. It's his turn to smirk.

"Easy, now. This is a workplace."

In her office, Helen lets me go ten minutes early with a wave of her pale hand, thick cut jewels glinting on her fingers. She doesn't even bother looking up from the dizzying spreadsheets she has split between two monitors.

"Don't call in sick tomorrow if you're hungover. Say the words, Frankie. Say: Helen, I'm a hungover wretch."

I peck her powdered cheek.

"Will do. In fact, I'll say it now: Helen, I won't be in tomorrow. I'll be a hungover wretch."

She snorts. "I'll see you in two days. Make good decisions."

"No promises." I bump the door open with my hip.

Maybe I should keep it tame. Lay off the street food and alcohol. Act like a responsible adult with an apartment and job.

But what's the point of having three bossy, overprotective boyfriends if I can't let loose once in a while?

* * *

"Try this."

Kingston spoons some kind of curry into my mouth. It's sweet and spicy, so hot my nose starts to run, and flavors explode across my tongue. I groan, wiping my nose on the back of my hand.

"What is that?"

He beams. "No damn clue."

He tries to feed Jamie next, reaching across my lap, but he bats him away, eyes wide and alarmed.

"Do you know how fucking red I'll turn if I eat that?"

Kingston snickers. "That's the point, sweetheart."

I draw my feet up onto the stone wall we've picked to sit and watch the parade, their bickering washing over me.The music thrums down the street, wrapping around the crowd, sending hips swaying and fingers tapping. Somewhere nearby, someone's cooking barbecue, the smell of smoke and hickory wafting through the air.

It's perfect. I feel so damn alive.

Tessa walks past with a group from the riverboat, a vision in feathers and beads and bare skin. She whoops and waves at us, and I grin and wave back. I'll be picking bits of feather out of our sofa for weeks.

"What do you think?" Jamie leans down to murmur in my ear, his breath tickling my skin.

I rest my head on his shoulder. "Way better than last year. Though it was fun watching you beat up that banker."

"What? You—" Jamie cuts himself off, shaking his head. Gabriel stands and smirks at me, shark-like.

"Shall we play hide and seek again this year, Frankie?"

I shift on the wall and bite my lip. There's a dark glint in Gabriel's eyes, and I bet running from him would be a whole different thing altogether. A string of places I could hide—places I'd like him to find me—scroll past my eyes and I smile.

"What are the rules?"

Gabriel cocks his head. "There are no rules."

Jamie mutters under his breath, shaking his head. Kingston shoves the last spoonful of curry in his mouth, rising and dusting his hands.

"I'm in," he says, mouth full. "I want to play hunt-the-Frankie."

Jamie curses, louder this time, then nods.

"Fine." He pushes to his feet and turns to me, face stern. "I have a score to settle."

I squeeze my thighs together, looking at them one by one. I don't know who I want to find me first more. Gabriel's shoulders are relaxed, the only hint of his excitement in the dark glint to his eyes. Jamie rolls up his sleeves, eyes flicking up at me from under his brows. And Kingston bounces on his toes, like he's about to chase me like the hounds of hell.

I hold up a finger. "Two things. I need a head start. And you can't work together."

Jamie and Gabriel both scoff at the same time, then exchange side-eyes.

"We won't."

"All right." I'm practically bouncing on the wall, adrenaline buzzing through my blood. That first week we met was a lot of things, but dull was definitely not one of them. "Close your eyes."

They do it, all three of them, and I take the opportunity to kiss them one by one. I scrape my teeth over Gabriel's throat; suck a kiss below Kingston's ear, and nibble on Jamie's bottom lip. It's him I murmur to, our lips still touching.

"Count to one hundred, then come find me."

He grins. "Better run and hide."

Author's Note

Thanks for reading Spring Kings! I hope you enjoyed it. Writing it has given me the weirdest urge to run away on a riverboat. Also to go on a cheesy ghost walk through a graveyard...

If you enjoyed Spring Kings, please consider leaving a review! It's a huge help to new authors, and is excellent for karma :D

This book officially wraps up the Year of the Harem collection. Don't forget to check out the other seasons for more reverse harem goodness, and have a wonderful year yourself!

Kayla xx

Let's keep in touch!

If you enjoy my work and you want to be the first to know what I'm up to, please consider signing up for my newsletter! I send bonus content, book recommendations, cover reveals, and other goodies twice a month.

Subscribers also get a free download of my *Lords of Summer* prequel: *Before the Fall.*

Here's a sneak peek…

* * *

She's here.

She's arrived in the quad.

Layla Mackenzie.

I glance up between the curtain of my dark hair, my elbows resting on my knees. It's still early September, barely the start of second year, and summer hasn't relinquished its hold. The air is warm—warm enough that the students dotted around the grass and on the benches are still in t-shirts. They kick back, legs stretched out, laughing in groups or studying solo.

It's the beginning of the year, and everything feels heavy with promise. With potential.

Layla picks her way across the grass, stepping over outstretched legs and winding between abandoned backpacks.

She nods at a few of the groups; waves at a couple of solo students. They wave back, calling out her name, inviting her to join them.

Everyone loves Layla. What's not to love? The buttery sunshine dances over her, drawing deep bronze highlights out of her dark red hair.

Fuck.

No one makes an ass of me like Layla. I look at her creamy skin, her sweet, cheeky smile, and all words dry up in my throat. The only thing that hurts worse than looking at her is not looking at her, and every second in her presence is a sweet torture. And all the while that I'm here dying, she has no clue. She probably doesn't even know my name.

It doesn't matter. She's too good, too happy for me to let myself get near. I'm not built for sweet girls, nor for holding hands on the way to class. No gentle kisses in the sunshine. No: if I got my callused hands on her, she'd come away stained.

I couldn't bear that.

As if she can hear my thoughts, Layla glances in the direction of my bench, and I drop my gaze to my hands. I run a thumb over the opposite knuckle, back and forth, feigning interest in the scars flecking my skin.

It was a rough summer back home. It always is. Rough, but satisfying: endless days of back-breaking labor, sweetened by the jokes between workers, and at the end of the season, the tangible results. Our family ranch was built on sweat and blood, started from the ground up. It's bigger now, one of the most successful in the state, but the demands are bigger too.

The blood and sweat never go away; it's a yearly tithe, and we pay it.

I risk a glance at Layla again, to see which lucky bastards she decided to sit with, but she's gone from the center of the quad. My head jerks up fully, and I whip my gaze around, only to find her sat a few feet away on the next bench over.

My heart speeds in my chest, hammering against my rib cage, and my mouth goes dry.

Fuck. This is the problem: this is what she does to me.

She makes me foolish, reckless. Raw.

Layla sees me looking around like I've lost my puppy, because of course she does - she's not blind. I lose sight of her for fifteen seconds and the panic practically bleeds from my pores. She's not the only one who notices either; the nearest group lazing on the grass are watching me curiously too.

I let my eyes meet hers for a split second, then slide my gaze away, like I'm still looking. Like I haven't found who I'm searching for.

I swear she deflates just a little.

Fuck. I want to go over there, to just snatch up my stuff and march over to sit beside her. I want to snuff out any doubt in her mind that she's the one I'm looking for—she's always the one.

Every day, I come to the quad during lunch for the sole purpose of seeing her. I sit on this bench, or lay out on the grass—that part isn't important. What's important is that she always comes too, usually alone. And she always seems to pick out a spot near me to sit.

I don't kid myself that she does it on purpose. We've barely said ten words to each other, even since Eli started bringing her to hang out with our group. But maybe—subconsciously—she's as drawn to me as I am to her. Maybe she feels the same pull, the same fishing hook in her gut tugging her towards me.

The only relief is when she's near. Then I can breathe again.

God, I sound fucking insane.

See, this is why I can't bother the girl. If I say any of this shit out loud, if I tell her how she makes me feel, I'll be locked away in a padded room and they'll be right to do it.

Better to enjoy these stolen moments with her, then force myself back to my day.

It's not like I can tell the others, either. Eli, Jasper and Nate. I've seen the way they look at her too. We're all as fucking bad as each other.

Jealousy curls through me, hot and vicious, whenever any of my friends talk to her. And though they've never acknowledged it, they seek her out almost as much as I do. At least once a week, I'll see Jasper stood behind her in line at the campus coffee shop, leaning down with a smile curling his lips to murmur in her ear. His wavy blond hair slides forward, tickling at her cheek.

I see the shiver that runs up her spine, too. It makes me want to tear him away from her, to throw him through the huge glass window.

But when he catches up with me a few minutes later, coffee in hand, I always force a smile. What am I going to say, anyway? Hey, man, that's my dream woman that I never plan to speak to?

Nate and Eli are just as bad. Nate gets this feral glint in his eye whenever she's near, like he's putting out pheromones or some shit. A lot of girls are scared of Nate, with his buzzed head and the tattoos all over his arms and chest. But he makes Layla laugh with his savage words, the sound ringing bright between the pale stone buildings.

I long for the sound of her laugh even as I hate that I'm not the one to draw it from her.

Eli is the worst of all. He spoke to her first, got to know her in some tutorial group, so he thinks he has some kind of claim on her. It makes me want to fucking scream when he tucks an arm around her shoulders, possessive and sure.

I saw her first. I fucking craved her first.

I just never did anything about it.

Eli and Jasper round the corner to the quad, moving with confident strides. They laugh and talk as they walk, raising a hand each when they notice me. We found each other during orientation week of first year, Nate included. It was so fucking easy, like four jigsaw pieces slotting into place.

I've never had that before. Not with friends, and certainly not with family. What we have, the four of us—it's like breathing. Unconscious and vital.

Both of their eyes light up when they notice Layla on the next bench over. I have to remind myself then that these guys are brothers to me —that I can't lose my shit over a dumb surge of jealousy.

Then Eli strides straight past my bench to sit next to Layla. A dark curl falls over his forehead, and his eyes crinkle when he speaks.

No. No, he can't tuck her hair behind her ear—can't make her blush like that. I shoot a glance at Jasper to see what he thinks, but he's watching the two of them with heat in his gaze. I want to shake him, then rip Eli away from Layla and shake him too. Can't they see how wrong this is?

It should be me on that fucking bench.

I tried to stay away for so long. Since the first time I saw Layla, way back in October of first year. I thought I could protect us both by keeping away, but now she's everywhere I look, and my friends have set their sights on her.

Fuck that. I won't bow out without a fight.
Today is the day I tell Layla Mackenzie how I feel.

Teaser: The Naughty List

It all starts with a magazine article. *The Naughty List: a bucket list for bad girls.*

All her life, Addie Miller has been good.

The dutiful daughter. The supportive best friend. The helpful tenant.

And where has it got her? Alone for Christmas, working in an elf costume and cleaning the little Russian old lady's apartment upstairs. Addie's only selfish pleasure is tormenting the prickly, gorgeous guy next door.

Well, no more.

It's time to say no. Time to grow a pair. Time to be *bad.*

And time to tempt her hot, grumpy neighbor out of his apartment and into her life.

The Naughty List is a steamy holiday romance with a guaranteed HEA. Contains mulled wine, embarrassing grandparents, weaponized mistletoe, and a hot nerd so tender he'll melt the frostiest of hearts.

Available now on Amazon.

Read on for a sneak peek...

* * *

I dropped the cardboard box on the parquet tiles, strands of tinsel and cracked baubles scattering over the floor.

"Crap."

I sighed and glanced around, but the lobby was empty. No friendly faces in sight. Just glowing orange lights fixed on old-fashioned wallpaper, the bank of mailboxes, and the sweeping staircase.

Fine. Okay. I'd spent all week at work untangling string lights and decking out store mannequins in Santa hats. I could do another hour.

I crouched low, my striped elf leggings straining, and swept the halo of glittery destruction into my hand. When I'd agreed to help decorate the apartment building, I'd pictured a team effort. At the very least, the landlord Mr Henson getting his burly hands dirty. But no—I'd just spent thirty minutes dragging boxes of ancient decorations up from the basement, their cardboard disintegrating in my grip.

"Motherf—"

A shard of cracked bauble sliced my thumb, a bead of glossy crimson blood welling up in the cut. I shook my hand, cursing under my breath, and glared at the sparkling mess on the tiles.

I couldn't leave it. Someone might step on it—slice their foot—and every time someone passed this stretch, they'd see this mess and think of me. A sickly feeling churned in my stomach.

I hated disappointing people.

My phone buzzed in my pocket, vibrating through my thin elf's smock against my hip. I fished it out, wincing as a spot of blood stained the fabric, and pressed it to my ear.

"Hello? Mr Henson?"

"Are you done yet, Addie?"

His gravelly old voice was even blunter over the phone. Usually, when I passed him in the halls, he at least grunted hello. But from the tone in my ear, you'd think I was the world's biggest pain in his ass, not his pro bono decorator.

"Um. No. I just started."

The sigh rattled down my speakers.

"How long will it take?"

Indignation straightened my spine, and I leveled a glare at the hallway wall.

"Much less time if you help, Mr Henson."

He cleared his throat, and when he spoke again he was all cheery bluster.

"Oh, no rush! No rush. You'll do a bang-up job."

I rolled my eyes, tipping to the side to sit down and save my burning thighs. It was always like this: Halloween, Valentine's Day, the Fourth of July. Mr Henson sniffed out my compulsive need to please like a shark scenting blood in the water. And he got me decorating and baking and—one time—collecting tips for his 'hard work'.

Please.

Each holiday, I promised myself it was the last time. I told Mr Henson too, my voice polite but firm.

But then I heard the other residents *ooh* and *ahh* over the decorations; saw Mrs Petrova steal a paper Valentine's rose when she thought no one was looking.

And I melted. I couldn't help it. I was the world's biggest sucker.

"Addie Miller. You cannot be serious."

I flapped my hand at my best friend as she stopped on the bottom step of the staircase. Mira crossed her arms, leaning against the wooden banister, staring into the pile of boxes with a wrinkled nose.

"Are there rats in there? I bet there are rats."

I shushed her, turning my head so I could hear Mr Henson grumble on. Something about lifting the residents' spirits and the rent going up.

Crap. I screwed my eyes shut, letting my forehead thunk against my knees. No way could I afford another price hike; not when I went to work in stripy leggings and a hat with a bell.

"You know what, Mr Henson?" I sounded strangled. "I have to go."

"Oh? Yes, all right," he grumbled, though he seemed to be winding up for another rant. I hung up before he could get going again and tossed my phone to the floor.

"Rents are going up."

Mira hissed. "That fucker."

"Yup."

"He'd better be paying you for this."

I cringed. I was sat on the musty tiles, bleeding and covered in ancient glitter and an elf costume. Mira growled, twitching towards me like she wanted to strangle me.

"Are you for real? *Why*, Addie? You don't even like this shit!"

I eyed the boxes of decorations doubtfully. A ceramic angel with a chipped nose squinted back at me.

"I like Christmas..."

"This isn't festive." Mira stomped down the last step onto the tiles, lashing out to kick the nearest box. "This is old, grimy and disgusting. And you're not helping, you're compulsively trying to please a man you hate."

She had me there. I sighed and gripped the banister, tugging myself to my feet.

"It's not for Mr Henson. Not really. Mrs Petrova told me the other day that this is her favorite time of year. That the holidays keep her going."

Mira hummed, a glint in her eye. "Oh, yeah? What were you doing with Mrs Petrova?"

"I was—" I cut myself off, glaring at her. Fine: I was *helping*, cleaning up her apartment while she rested her old feet. "We were hanging out."

"Uh-huh."

She wasn't buying it. Not for a second. Mira knew me better than anyone—Hell, I spent the first six months of our friendship offering to help, to watch over her laundry in the machine or water her plants, before she snapped and told me to cut it out.

I turned away, swinging my long, dark hair over my shoulder as I bent down so she wouldn't see my flaming cheeks.

Scraggly tinsel. Splotchy baubles. String lights with half the bulbs missing. I rummaged deeper, determined to find something worth winding around the banister. The scent of mildew wafted up from the box.

"I'm going to stage an intervention, you know."

I grunted.

"This isn't healthy."

I flapped a hand at her without looking.

"Shoo, naysayer. Or get your hands dirty."

I fully expected the thud of Mira's biker boots on the stairs. Instead, a pair of manicured hands plunged into the box beside mine, and I hid a smile.

"Don't take this as approval."

"I won't."

"I still think this is pathetic."

"Noted."

"I'm just—oh, fuck." Mira slowly withdrew one hand, grimacing at the sticky residue coating her palm. She shook her head, hard, like she was snapping out of a trance, and shot to her full height. "Nope. No way. Screw this six ways to Sunday. You're on your own."

I grinned, braiding frosty white tinsel around the banister as her enraged footsteps echoed along the floor above. The slam of her door echoed through the hallway, and then it was just me and the rustle of glittery plastic.

* * *

I dusted my hands off and stepped back, surveying my masterpiece. The lobby *sparkled*: glass snowflakes spun beneath the sconces on the walls, and colored lights winked from potted shrubs. A traditional wooden calendar counted down the days of December, placed on top of the mailboxes and surrounded by frosted pine cones.

There was holly. There were candles—battery powered, but still. And clutched in my hand was the final touch: a sprig of mistletoe.

I cocked my head and surveyed the lobby. I'd spread bits and pieces through the halls, but this right here was the main event. A burst of color, with pinpricks of string lights glinting like stars.

The mistletoe rustled under my fingertips. Pearly white berries nestled in the leaves, just like Mrs Petrova's favorite pair of earrings.

Where to hang a sprig of mistletoe?

The obvious place would be the entrance way, or somewhere near the mailboxes. But visions of the creepy guy on the third floor stopped me from hanging it there.

No. Better to keep this low key. The female residents would thank me.

There was Mira's door, of course, but she was the last person to need help getting kisses. She was beautiful, with her coppery shoulder-length hair and plump mouth, and she damn well knew it. But more than that, Mira did not give a crap about what anyone thought of her—least of all men.

Apparently that was powerfully erotic.

After Mira, my closest friend in the building was Mrs Petrova on the top floor. The tiny, spherical old woman was stooped with age, but her eyes were sharp and her mind was quick. She'd cackle to see mistletoe hanging from her door frame, then swat me with her broom.

Already snickering, I clutched the sprig tight and marched towards the staircase. But at the last second, my feet veered to the right, rounding the banister and plunging down the hallway. My own apartment was down here—past the reach of the sconce lights, cloaked in shadows and right next to the laundry room. Plenty of times, I startled awake in bed after midnight, woken by the clash and groan of the machines.

That dark, noisy apartment was the only reason I could afford this building.

That, and the tiny fact that my bathroom was three doors

away down the hall.

I didn't head towards my apartment. It would be tragically desperate to hang mistletoe on my own door frame.

No. I had another target in mind.

He'd hate it. He'd be so, so pissed. I knew that, and yet I couldn't help myself. I paused in front of my neighbor's door, smirking at the peephole.

If helping was my biggest addiction, messing with Lucas Murphy was a close second. He was terminally grumpy, a malevolent presence looming over the mailboxes or stalking through the halls. In all the two years we'd spent living a few feet away from each other, he'd never once smiled at me. Not even when I knocked on his door offering cookies, or took delivery of parcels for him.

He just dragged his imperious gaze from my head to my boots, then wrinkled his nose in distaste.

Ass.

Yes, Lucas Murphy could use all the romantic help he could get. I was doing him a favor. A good Christmas deed. I ran my palm up his door frame, scanning for a hook or nail to hang my little gift.

"What are you doing?"

The deep voice made me jump. I spun around, hiding the mistletoe behind my back like a guilty toddler.

"Nothing."

"Nothing?" Lucas scowled at me, his blue eyes flicking over my shoulder to check his door. "Do you always stroke strangers' doors?"

"We're hardly strangers."

The words were out of my mouth before my brain could stop them. I winced, watching the storm clouds gather on my neighbor's face, and backed up a step until my shoulder blades hit his door.

"Oh, really? Do we work together?" Lucas advanced a step, crowding me against the wood. His shoulders were deceptively broad under those shirts.

"No."

"Do we get drinks? Go to movies?"

"No. And no."

"So we're not friends. Not colleagues. Barely casual acquaintances, wouldn't you say?"

I nodded, glaring up at him with thinly disguised loathing. Man, I hated this guy. I wanted to ruffled his black hair; knock his glasses askew. I wanted to drag him into my bathroom and give him a swirlie.

"So what, Miss Miller, were you doing by my door?"

I held up the mistletoe, dangling it between us. Lucas reared back like I'd shown him a snake, eyes widening in alarm.

Ha. Vicious triumph shot through me.

"Just decorating for the holidays. Did you see the lobby?"

He cleared his throat, recovering. "I did."

"What do you think?"

"Horrendous. If I wanted to live in a grotto, I'd move to the North Pole."

Ah, Lucas. He was consistent. I rolled my eyes, my evil prank foiled, and pushed off his door. He could be an unbearable Grinch if he wanted—I'd expect nothing less. But Mrs Petrova would appreciate the mistletoe, and I still had four moldy boxes to drag back to the basement.

"Well, this has been fun and all, but I need to get going."

"Running late for Santa?"

I frowned, confused, then looked down at my stupid elf

costume, all the way to the little bells on my curly-toed boots. Shit. I opened my mouth, ready to blurt something clever, but Lucas' door closed in my face with a snap.

Asshole. Every time, every *single time,* he always got the last freaking word.

I gritted my teeth. Counted backwards from ten. Then forced out a slow breath.

Who cared if Lucas Murphy was an ass? I had decorations to finish, a shift to go to, and a bargain-bin bottle of wine to drink with Mira later.

Unlike Lucas-Loner-Murphy, I had a life to live.

About the Author

Kayla Wren is a British author who writes steamy New Adult romance. She loves Reverse Harem, Enemies-to-Lovers, and Forbidden Love tropes.

Kayla writes prickly men with hearts of gold, secretly-sexy geeks, and—best of all—she's ALWAYS had a thing for the villains.

You can connect with me on:

https://www.kaylawrenauthor.com

https://www.facebook.com/kaylawrenauthor

https://www.bookbub.com/authors/kayla-wren

Subscribe to my newsletter:

https://newsletter.kaylawrenauthor.com/beforethefall

Also by Kayla Wren

Lords of Summer

They tortured me all year at college.

Now I'm working the summer as their maid.

Lords of Summer is the first installment in the Year of the Harem collection.

Autumn Tricksters

The circus is smoke and mirrors. It's misfits and flames.

It's the place where tricksters come to play.

Autumn Tricksters is the second installment in the Year of the Harem collection.

Knights of Winter

We were only supposed to be here for two weeks, but the snowstorm traps us in the castle together.

Knights of Winter is the third installment in the Year of the Harem collection.

Printed in Great Britain
by Amazon